SAMMIE

To Jessie

Hope you enjoy

H. David Campbell

SAMMIE

H. DAVID CAMPBELL

SAMMIE

iUniverse books may be ordered through booksellers or by contacting:

iUniverse
1663 Liberty Drive
Bloomington, IN 47403
www.iuniverse.com
1-800-Authors (1-800-288-4677)

ISBN: 978-1-5320-8662-5 (sc)
ISBN: 978-1-5320-8682-3 (hc)
ISBN: 978-1-5320-8681-6 (e)

Print information available on the last page.

iUniverse rev. date: 10/25/2019

Contents

Chapter One

The O'Grady's Love for Boats

Sophia Larson and Cody O'Grady lived in Madison, Wisconsin. They both worked at the same school, Liberty Elementary, as new teachers. They met each other on their first day when they began teaching. They liked each other right away. A few days later, quite by accident, they met on the stairway of Miss Donavon's Apartment house where they both lived.

"Cody, I didn't know you lived here," Sophia remarked.

"Yes, Sophia, I live in 302. What apartment do you live in?"

"I live in 227. I can't believe we haven't run into each other before now."

They spent all of their free time together and quickly fell in love. They soon discovered that they both loved going to the lakes some weekends, having picnic lunches, and renting boats. They began to make new friends that also loved boating too.

It was just four months later in December that Sophia and Cody were married. They were now Mr. and Mrs. O'Grady.

After continually renting boats at the lake, Sophia commented, "Cody, let's buy a boat, please?"

"That's a great idea, Sophia. It will take a while to save up, but let's do it!"

The apartment house that Sophia and Cody lived in was a great place. Some of the other teachers from their school also rented there. One day they met Mrs. Gibson. She was an older woman that always loved to stop them to visit. She became like a loving grandmother to them. She invited them to dinner several times, knowing how busy they were as school teachers.

Sophia and Cody gave her a birthday present on her special day and also took her out to dinner. During the Christmas season, she invited them to help decorate her Christmas tree, and then went up to their apartment to help them. She was a real delight to have as a neighbor in their building.

The reason they loved living in Madison, Wisconsin, was because of the many lakes that were available for them to use when they would finally get their new boat. There are15,074 lakes that are named in Wisconsin, the largest being Mendota Lake.

It was September and the beginning of their 2nd year of teaching. One evening after dinner, Sophia approached Cody. "I have something to tell you."

"I'm listening, Sophia."

"We're going to have a baby. It will be some time this next May."

He was overjoyed and hugged and kissed her over and over again.

The year they took delivery of their new boat, they also had their new baby daughter.

Before she was born, Sophia suggested, "Cody, let's name our baby girl, Samantha. Do you like that name?"

"Yes, kind of, I guess," he responded.

"I know, Cody, her real name will be Samantha, but we'll call her *Sammie*!"

"Now that sounds good, Sophia. We'll call our daughter, *Sammie*. I like that nickname."

A few weeks before she was born, they would always head for one of the lakes to enjoy their new boat. They loved to barbecue at some of the neat parks around the lakes they would visit. They continued to make even more new friends.

The day finally arrived that Sophia had her beautiful baby. Cody sure was a proud father. Sophia so enjoyed staying home with Sammie for a few weeks.

Now with Sammie, their newborn baby in their lives, they wondered who they could find to tend her while they were away at school and gone for some weekends.

Mrs. Gibson heard that they were looking for someone to care for their baby. The very next day after they both came home from school, she went up and knocked on their door.

Sophia answered, "Well, hello, Mrs. Gibson. Come in!"

"I heard that you've been looking for someone to care for Samantha."

"Yes, we have been looking. We've been taking Sammie to one of those daycare places."

"What would you think about me taking care of her?" Mrs. Gibson asked.

"That would be wonderful, Mrs. Gibson. That's a pretty big job caring for a newborn."

Cody was nearby and heard them talking. "Mrs. Gibson, would you be up to doing something like this?"

"Yes, yes, I would!" she responded.

"You have the job, Mrs. Gibson. Promise to tell us if it's too much for you now," cried Sophia.

Mrs. Gibson loved Sammie so much. Her first six months were a challenge, but now it was a delight to care for

Sammie. She was the cutest baby Mrs. Gibson had ever seen.

Cody and Sophia took Sammie everywhere with them after their school day was over. On weekends when they would go with their friends to the lakes, Mrs. Gibson would care for her.

Soon, Sammie was two, and she was such a good baby, never giving them any trouble. They took a lot of videos and pictures of her.

Sophia and Cody were finishing another year as teachers. After school, Sophia commented. "Cody, we'll be out of school for the summer in just a week. I would very much like to go and visit your parents down on their citrus ranch. They have never seen their granddaughter."

"No, Sophia. You know I've never gotten along with my dad. They expected me to stay on the ranch, but I wanted to be a teacher. My father was disappointed that I didn't want to stay and work on his ranch. He did, however, finally agreed to pay for my college, which surprised me."

"You never wanted to communicate with either Simon or Davis. Don't you love and care at all about your brothers?"

"I remember your sending them all the announcement of Samantha's birth. Did you ever hear anything back from them, Sophia?"

"No, I didn't. I was disappointed about that, Cody."

"So, what makes you want to visit them now?"

Another year went whizzing by. Sophia was planning a big party for Sammie's third birthday, which was May 23rd. Teachers in their school and people in their building who had kids around Sammie's age were invited to her party.

The day finally came. Mrs. Gibson helped run all the activities with Sophia that she had planned for the kids. The party was a huge success. Their little Sammie was growing up.

After the party was over and everyone had left, Sammie asked, "Mommy, you said when I was three, you'd take me with you on the weekends. Can I go this weekend with you and Daddy, please?"

"Yes, Sammie, I did promise you that you could go with us some weekends, but not this weekend. We are having a special time with two of our friends that are launching their new boats."

"Well, then, will you take me the next weekend after that?" cried Sammie.

"Yes, my darling daughter, we will."

The weekend came, and Sammie was sad that she couldn't go with her parents but was looking forward to the following weekend when she would be able to go with them for sure.

As Cody and Sophia entered Mendota Lake Park, they saw only one of their friends who had brought their new boat to launch for the first time.

"Jason, your new boat is great. I love the color. Where are Jimmy and Lois?"

"They said that the weather didn't look favorable and that they would bring their new boat next week."

"Let me help you launch your new boat," exclaimed Cody.

"No, Cody, I don't think I will. Look to the west."

"That weather won't be here for another three or four more hours. I'm going to launch my boat."

"Are you sure, Cody? I don't think it's a good idea."

"It will be fine, Jason. We will only be out for an hour or so." He then hollered for Sophia.

"Cody, everyone seems to think boating today isn't a good idea. Maybe they're right," cried Sophia.

"Come on, Sophia, our boat is all ready to go. We'll only go for an hour."

Off they went. After about 45 minutes, Sophia said, "Cody, we need to head back. Those black clouds have come upon us a lot sooner than we thought. The wind is getting really bad too. I hope we can make it back, okay."

The winds were really bad, and high gusts of wind were rocking their boat, almost turning it over.

"Cody," exclaimed Sophia. "Those great gusts of wind are surely going to turn over our boat!"

She was right. Shortly afterward, the boat did turn over. Cody tried finding Sophia, but the huge waves and heavy winds were just too much for him. Soon both Cody and Sophia disappeared under the water.

Their friends, Jason and Cindy, watched for Cody and Sophia's boat. The weather was getting pretty bad. They hoped that they had put their craft into the shore. They never came back. Jason reported them as possibly lost, hoping he was wrong.

Meanwhile, back at their home, Mrs. Gibson was beginning to worry because they didn't come home, and it was getting dark. They were always home before dark. After eight, she knew something bad must have happened to them.

The next few days were awful. They never found their bodies, at least not yet. The authorities were contacting Cody's and Sophia's families to see who might want to take Sammie.

The authorities found that Cody had two brothers. Davis O'Grady, who lived in Morris, Minnesota, and Simon O'Grady who lived in Florida on a ranch with his parents, Samuel and Sadie O'Grady.

Sophia was an only child. Her parents, Rachel and William Larson, both lived in London and were professors at one of the large universities.

Both Cody's and Sophie's parents came to the funeral, as well as Cody's two brothers and their wives.

There wasn't very much conversation during or after the funeral. The only ones who were very friendly were Cody's two brothers, Simon, and Davis, along with their wives Hannah and Kate.

After the funeral, Simon made it known that his wife, Hannah, was to have a baby and that it would be hard for them to take Sammie.

Sophie's parents commented that taking Sammie would be impossible as busy as they both were.

Cody's parents said they would take Sammie if no one else wanted her.

Everyone began to wonder who would take care of Cody and Sophie's little Sammie. Then Davis, one of Cody's brothers, declared, "Kate and I will take her."

Davis and Kate O'Grady lived in Morris, Minnesota. They never had any children, so they thought raising Samantha would be wonderful for them.

Mrs. Gibson was broken-hearted, having to let Sammie go, but she knew that she would be with family. She would keep her until the courts settled things. The family then discussed cleaning out their apartment and what items they should keep for Sammie to have when she got older.

Chapter Two

Sammie's New Home

The authorities finally notified Davis and Kate O'Grady that they could take Sammie. Back in Morris, Minnesota, Davis, and Kate were happy to know that they would have Sammie. Davis was a police officer, and Kate was a caregiver for triplet girls. She thought adding Sammie wouldn't be too much more work than the three two-year-old girls. She informed the girl's mother, Kathy Hughes, about adding Sammie.

Kate and Davis were finally on their way to Madison, Wisconsin to get Sammie. On their way there, Davis commented, "Kate, I wonder how hard it will be for little Sammie to get used to us."

Davis and Kate hoped that they would be able to give Sammie the love that she would need at this terrible time in her life.

They finally arrived at Mrs. Donavon's apartment house. They went in and found apartment 232 and knocked on the door.

Mrs. Gibson opened the door. They saw Sammie clinging to Mrs. Gibson.

"Please, come in. I'm glad to see you have arrived safely." She then turned to Sammie, "Can you say hello?"

She just hid behind Mrs. Gibson.

"Come here, Sammie," Kate pleaded.

Mrs. Gibson led Sammie to Kate. Kate hugged her and told her, "Sammie, I'm so glad that you are coming to live with us now. I'm your Aunt Kate, and this is your Uncle Davis."

Sammie started crying and ran back to Mrs. Gibson. After an hour, Mrs. Gibson had all of her things ready to go.

Mrs. Gibson then addressed Sammie, "I may come to visit you soon. I'm going to miss you so much." She hugged her again and said her final good-bye.

It was 424 miles back to Morris, Minnesota. At least it was summer, and the weather was good. They knew that they would have to stop in Minneapolis on the way back. Kate held Sammie on her lap for the first two hours, hugging and kissing her. Sammie kept saying, "I want to go back to be with my Grammy."

When she was getting sleepy, Kate put her in a child seat, hoping she would go to sleep.

When they stopped in Minneapolis, they found a motel. It had a nice café. Sammie didn't want to eat, but she finally did have some macaroni and cheese. She then said, "I want some ice cream."

That night she slept between Davis and Kate. She snuggled up to Kate. She thought maybe she was beginning to accept them a little.

They finally arrived back in Morris. Davis had always hated big cities. After they got married, Kate and Davis looked and looked for a charming little town that they would love to live in someday soon.

They finally found the right place, Morris, Minnesota. It had a beautiful town square with a lovely park in the middle. It had a movie theater, a drug store, a hardware store, a dentist, a vet, a small motel with a café, a small grocery store, a small clothing store, a post office, and an elementary school. It was perfect for them.

They were glad to be back home in Morris. While Davis unpacked the car, Kate took Sammie into their house. She wanted to show Sammie the bedroom they had prepared for her.

She looked at it and ran back to Kate, shouting, "I want to stay with you and Uncle Davis in your bedroom, please?"

She continued crying and hugging Kate. Just then, Davis came in carrying a lot of their things. "Why is she crying, Kate?"

"She doesn't like her room. I guess it's just too much for her to take in right now. She wants to sleep with us like we did last night. I hope that's okay with you, Davis."

"Yes, Kate, I won't mind at all. I'm glad that she wants to be close to us. I have fallen for this dear sweet little girl."

He continued, "Kate, I think we should adopt this precious child as our very own daughter. I'm pretty sure we can legally do it."

"Really, Davis, we can do that? Then I think that's what we should start pursuing, right away. I'm so sorry I was unable to have any children, but now we have Sammie."

"Won't it be great to have her call us Mother and Father? It seems like a dream to me, Kate."

In the morning, Kate got Sammie fed and dressed. She was hoping she would like the triplets.

As Kate and Sammie entered the triplet's house, Kathy Hughes, the girl's mother, exclaimed, "So this is Sammie. What a darling girl, Kate. I hope all goes well with the girls today. See you later."

The triplet's mother, Kathy, was a hospital administrator in a nearby town, with responsibility for three other small clinics in the area.

The triplets were identical, and even Kate, at times, would get them mixed up. Their names were Jenifer, Lexie, and Cami.

At first, Sammie would stand a little away from the girls. Kate finally grabbed Cami and took her over to Sammie.

"Sammie...Cami needs a hug." Sammie didn't want to. Cami then hugged Sammie. Then Jenifer and Lexie wanted a hug from Sammie too. Sammie then reluctantly embraced the other two.

Sammie then noticed that the triplets had a lot of their dolls out to play with that morning. Sammie loved playing with dolls. She made her way over to the triplets and began playing with them.

Kate smiled and thought, "I'm sure everything will be fine now."

Cami was the only one of the triplets who was talking a little, so Sammie and Cami bonded. Somehow, Sammie could tell the girls apart better than Kate could.

That evening when they returned home, Kate had some cute children's DVD'S to watch with Sammie.

As they were watching the DVDs, Davis returned, and he was smiling. "Kate, I have good news. I have started all the paperwork for Sammie's adoption. It will take a while, but I can hardly wait until she's all ours."

At night, Sammie still loved to snuggle up with Davis and Kate. Kate was hoping she would want to start sleeping in her own room. Sammie was also starting to eat her meals with them without any problems now.

It took a while, but the adoption was finally complete. Davis and Kate were delighted that Sammie was still so young, not quite four yet, because this would make the transition easier for them all. It wasn't long before she started to think of them as her mother and father.

Before they knew it, Sammie was now finally sleeping in her own room. The triplets that Kate cared for were three and were all talking now, and this made things a lot easier for Kate.

Next year, Sammie would be going to kindergarten, and the triplets would be going to pre-school. Kate was looking forward to that. With the next year finally here, having the triplets in school for a half-day and Sammie for the full day of kindergarten was great.

As Kate looked at her calendar, she thought, how could another year have slipped by already? Sammie was almost six and would be going into the first grade, and the triples would be going to kindergarten for the whole day! What would she do all day? Kate found out that the school was looking for help in their kindergarten classes. She applied and got the job. It was perfect combining her care of the girls and being in school with them as well.

Kate was so pleased that Sammie loved the triplets and was so close to them now. Sammie did find another special friend in her first-grade class. Her friend's name was Chloe.

When Chloe would come over to the triplets house after school, the triplets were a little jealous, especially Cami, but Chloe was such a loving, sweet girl that the triplets soon loved having Chloe visit them when she could.

Time was passing so quickly. Sammie was now seven and in the second grade. The triplets were six and going into the first grade.

It was a Wednesday evening, and Sammie's father was about to tell them about a surprise he had for them during their time at dinner.

"This Saturday, I'm taking you and your mother to St. Cloud. It's only 93 miles from here, less than a two-hour drive. Sammie, you'll love St. Cloud. It has a big mall and lots of places to eat. Your mom and I usually went to St. Cloud every couple of months, so we've sure missed going."

"Yes, I have missed going too, Davis. With having Sammie and trying to keep the house up and preparing meals, it was difficult thinking about taking the time to go," commented Kate.

"Daddy, can I take my friend, Chloe, please?"

"Yes, it would be nice for you to have a friend to come with us. You run over to Chloe's house and ask her parents."

Chloe only lived just four houses down the street. Sammie ran down and opened the door, saying, "Knock, knock, it's Sammie!"

Everyone in Morris knew everyone. No one ever locked their doors.

"Oh, hi, Mrs. Green," Sammie shouted, "My daddy said he's taking me and my mom to St. Cloud this Saturday. Can Chloe come with us, please?"

"Why, yes, I'm sure you and Chloe will love St. Cloud. It's a wonderful place to visit. Chloe's up in her room, Sammie. You can go up and give her the good news."

"Thank you, Mrs. Green," cried Sammie.

She dashed up the stairs. "Chloe, this Saturday, my family is taking me to visit St. Cloud, and I just asked your mom if you could come with us, and she said, yes!"

"Really, really and truly!" she yelled.

Saturday came, and they left about 8:00 a.m. On the way to St. Cloud, the girls had fun singing and being silly in the back seat. They got there just as the mall was opening.

"Wow, Daddy, I never saw such a wonderful place!" cried Sammie.

"Is anyone hungry? How about some ice cream, girls?" asked her father.

"Sammie, let's get you some new clothes," remarked Kate, her mother. "Chloe can help you pick out some."

Chloe did help in selecting some of the clothes for Sammie. She was a little jealous, not being able to get some clothes too. She was surprised when Kate exclaimed, "Chloe, you may pick out any new dress that you like."

"Really, Mrs. O'Grady? I can pick out *any* new dress I want?"

"Yes, Chloe, you may."

Sammie and Chloe were so happy shopping for new clothes for school. The girls finally located a beautiful dress for Chloe.

"Girls, it's time for lunch. Let's go to the big food court. You may pick anything you like to eat for your lunch," exclaimed Kate.

After a great lunch, it was time for them to return to Morris. The girls never had this much fun before. They arrived back home around 4:00 p.m.

Sammie loved living in Morris, Minnesota. She could see why her mom and dad loved Morris too. It was great knowing just about everyone in town.

Chapter Three

Nothing Stays the Same

Sammie's eighth birthday was approaching. Her birthday was May 23rd, and the weather was usually starting to be better at this time of year.

When Davis got home from work one evening, he asked if Rachel and William Larson, Sammie's grandparents who lived in London, had sent their usual gift and card for Sammie as they did every year.

"Yes, Davis, it arrived by special delivery as always. I wish they would come for a visit. We certainly can't afford to take Sammie to London."

"I know they keep saying they would like to come. Sammie told me she would like to meet them. She has their picture in her bedroom," remarked Davis.

When Sammie's grandparents would call her, she would always run to her bedroom to get their picture.

Davis and Kate wanted to do something really special for her eighth birthday. Davis thought about Mrs. Gibson back in Madison, Wisconsin. They hadn't heard anything from her for quite a while, and they wondered if she was still alive. Davis had a phone number for her and hoped it was still good. He called, and she answered.

"Hello, is this Mrs. Gibson?"

"Yes, who's calling?"

"This is Davis O'Grady. How are you? It's been quite a while since we've heard from you. Sammie is having a birthday party. She will be turning eight this year. Would you like to come?"

"I'd like to, but I can't afford it. I've lost my late husband's pension, so I have very little money to live on now, Davis."

"We'll be happy to pay for the bus trip both ways if you'll come."

"Really? I will come! I'd love to see how Samantha has grown."

"Mrs. Gibson, we still are calling her, Sammie. She likes everyone to call her that."

Mrs. Gibson did come, and Sammie did remember her. She had a picture of her in her bedroom that she saw every day. She had a wonderful time with Mrs. Gibson.

A few months went by, and it was late one September evening when Kate heard someone knocking at their door.

"Who is the world would be calling this late in the evening?" she wondered.

It was Marty, her husband's friend, from the police station where they both worked.

"Kate, your husband's been shot. He was called down to Benson City by their police department because some families down there were fighting and shooting at each other. He tried getting them to talk to him, and they shot him."

"Is he okay, though?" shouted Kate.

"No, Kate, he didn't make it. He's gone."

Sammie heard them talking and screamed, "No, no, no, it can't be true!" She then ran to Kate, who was crying too.

Chloe came over as soon as she heard. She slept with Sammie every night, trying to comfort her.

Kate called the O'Grady's in Florida to let them know about what had happened to ––Davis, their son. They all came to the funeral. Kate couldn't believe they came. Samuel O'Grady, Davis's father, was crying at the funeral. Simon, Samuel's only other son now, looked sad as well. Sadie, Davis's mother, was holding her own.

The police force in Morris and the people there in town all honored Davis. It was a large funeral with many speakers.

After the funeral, Sadie pulled Kate aside. "Kate, we all talked after you called us about Davis. We all feel very guilty for all the years we have been separated from you and Davis and about not seeing this beautiful granddaughter of ours."

Kate then commented, "It was because Cody and Davis didn't want to stay on the citrus ranch, and wanted to follow their own path, right?"

"Yes, that's right, Kate. My husband is a very proud man, and it hurt him deeply to see two of his sons leave the ranch. He now knows that it was very wrong of him to have isolated himself from his sons. Now the two of them are gone," Sadie sighed.

"How do *you* feel about isolating your sons from you, Sadie? Couldn't you have done something to connect with them?"

"I wanted to so badly, but my husband forbade me to ever connect with them, so my hands were tied. But now, Samuel, Simon, and I want you to come and live with us in Florida on our citrus ranch."

"What! How can you ask that of us? Is this to cover up your *guilt* for all the years you have avoided us?"

Sadie looked down at the floor and then responded, "I guess maybe we're trying to ask for your forgiveness. As Christians, we believe in forgiving one another. I know this may be very hard for you to do, but please think about coming to live on our citrus ranch."

Sadie then gave Kate a big kiss and hug.

"If I'm even going to consider this, Sadie, I want to hear your husband tell me he's sorry about his past actions and *does* want us to come. And it would be great to hear this from Simon too. I want to hear this from *all* of you before you leave to go back to Florida."

After the funeral, Sammie and Chloe went back to Sammie's house, where the neighbors had prepared food for the family members and some of their special close friends who had come to the funeral. Sammie and Chloe stayed in Sammie's room the whole time. She wouldn't make an appearance at all. She just wanted everyone to leave.

After everyone did leave, except for her grandparents and Simon and his wife, Hannah, Kate asked Sammie to come into the living room. She did so very reluctantly.

Her grandmother held out her arms. "Come here, Samantha."

Sammie was clinging to Kate and wouldn't go to her grandmother. She also just looked at her grandfather and Simon. Soon they all began to leave.

Sadie then commented as they were departing, "Kate, we hope to be hearing from you before we leave. We do all love you."

After they left, Sammie inquired, "Mom, did you call my grandparents in London?"

"No, Sammie, I didn't. They aren't part of the O'Grady family."

"I think they should know what's happened. Maybe we could go to London to live with them."

Kate did call her other grandparents, and Sammie talked for a long time. They told her to keep them advised as to what her mother had decided to do.

That night, Chloe slept with Sammie again. The next day after school, the triplets gave Sammie many hugs and continually wanted to be by her side to comfort her.

Chapter Four

A Change?

The very next morning their phone rang. Kate ran to answer it. "Kate, this is Sadie. We would like you to come to the motel at noon and have lunch with us so that we can talk."

"I'll be there, Sadie."

She began to realize that Davis's parents and his brother, Simon, and his wife were the only family she had now. She also began to know that with just her income, she wouldn't be able to support herself and Sammie. She would receive some social security benefits, but it was still a drop in her income.

Noon was approaching, and Kate was nervous. What if things got heated and she was to walk out on them? What would she do then? Maybe she could take in some people to rent rooms in her house, or move in with one of her single friends and share the expenses.

As she entered 'Jared's Eating Place,' she saw the four of them sitting in the back of the restaurant. "I guess that was because they wanted us to have some privacy," she concluded to herself

They all stood up as Kate approached. She was amazed to hear Davis's father personally invite her to sit next to him, which she did.

Samuel spoke first. "Kate, my dearest daughter-in-law, I have been up all night walking the streets of Morris. I have never shed that many tears in my whole life. I now realize what I missed not staying close to my sons, who now are both gone. Please, my dear sweet girl, can you forgive a hard-hearted old man? I hope I'm not that man anymore."

He reached for her with tears streaming down his face. Kate had tears running down her face as well. They both embraced each other.

"Samuel, I feel that you are a changed man. I do forgive you. I'm so sad that we missed all those years that we could have been a close family."

Simon then spoke. "Kate, I've always missed both of my brothers a lot, but I also needed to grant my father's wishes too. I wrote many letters to both of my brothers but couldn't get the courage to send them. I want you to know that my wife, Hannah, and I welcome you and Sammie into our family with open arms."

Sadie then stood and then walked over to Kate, and they hugged. "I'm so glad you have forgiven this stubborn family and that you will become part of our family now."

Kate added, "Now I'm wondering about how Sammie will react when she hears that we will be moving to Florida? I'll try to explain to her about our meeting here this afternoon."

Samuel added, "Kate, we'll be leaving here in about an hour. We will make all the arrangements for your move to the ranch. We'll pay for everything so you won't have to worry about money."

As Kate left the restaurant, her head was spinning. *"How would she* explain all of this to Sammie?" she wondered.

Later, Kate made her way to the school as it was time that school would be over.

Every day after school was over, the triplets and Sammie always waited for Kate to come and walk them all back to the triplet's house, but today she was early and waiting for them. When the triplets came out of their school and saw that Kate was waiting for them, they, of course, came running to her for their hugs.

On the way back, Kate told Sammie, "I met with the O'Grady's this afternoon, but I don't want to talk about it until we're back home."

Later, when they had gotten home, Kate expressed, "Come over here, Sammie, and sit down beside me. My meeting with the O'Grady's wasn't what I thought it would be at all."

"So was it better or worse than what you thought, Mother?"

"It was wonderful, Sammie! Your grandfather told me that he had been wrong all these years, and now realized that he'd lost two of his sons and that he wouldn't ever be able to tell them how sorry he was. He asked me to forgive him and said that he would be a different man now."

"Mom, did you forgive him?"

"Yes, Sammie, I did. Then, Sadie, your grandmother, got up and we hugged. She also wanted me to forgive her for not trying harder to resolve their family problems."

"Simon was the last, saying how much he always missed his brothers and now he is welcoming you and me into their family with open arms."

"So, what are we going to do now?"

"How would you like to move to Florida?"

"We can't, Mom. All my friends are here! We know everyone in town. How can we leave such a *perfect* place like Morris!" she said with tears now running down her face.

"Sammie, now that your dad isn't with us anymore, I can't support us with just my wages. Your grandparents have invited us to live on their citrus ranch. They grow oranges, grapefruit, and tangerines. It's a large ranch and very beautiful. They don't have any snow there either. It's like summer most of the time."

"I *won't* go, Mother! I'll just stay here with Chloe. *You* go to Florida!" She then ran to her room, crying.

After almost two hours, she came out of her room. "Well, Mom, maybe it wouldn't be so bad. What if we don't like it there, can we come back to Morris?"

"No, I'm afraid that the citrus ranch is where you'll be growing up. I'm sure you'll make new friends there. Your Grandpa Samuel will be sending us the tickets that we will need to get to the citrus ranch, and he is also paying for moving all of our things to Florida."

Sammie then called her grandparents in London and told them about moving to her other grandparent's big citrus ranch in Florida, and she said she hoped they would soon plan on coming to see them.

After Davis's death, the town wasn't surprised to hear that Kate and Sammie were moving out of Morris to Florida. The whole town then planned a big going away party for them.

Chloe was so sad that her best friend was leaving. She helped Sammie pack her things. Both girls were very teary-eyed.

"Chloe, my grandfather is wealthy. He is paying for us to move to Florida. I bet he would pay for you to come and see me in Florida."

"Really, that would be so neat to go so far to see you, Sammie!"

It was Friday evening, and they had set up everything in their big town hall for Kate's and Sammie's going away party. Everyone in Morris was sad to see them leaving. It was a wonderful thing the town had done for them.

Saturday morning had arrived, and so did the moving truck. It didn't take long to load their few things.

One of Kate's friends, Robin, drove them to the St. Cloud Airport to catch their plane. It would be a long flight to Florida.

Chapter Five

On Their Way to the O'Grady's Citrus Ranch

After saying their good-byes to Robin, they entered the airport. Some nice porter helped them check-in and told them where their plane would be departing.

Sammie ran to the big window where she could see the big plane that would be taking them to Florida. "Look, Mom, look how *big* the plane is!" she shouted.

"Yes, it certainly is big, all right. I've never been on an airplane before, and I know you haven't either. Are you afraid to go on this plane, Sammie?"

"No, I'm not going to be afraid at all. I think it's going to be exciting flying way up *high* in the clouds. Are you going to be afraid to fly in this airplane, Mom?"

"Yes, Sammie, I am. Maybe you could help me to be braver than I am now."

Soon they heard a lady calling for the passengers to line up to board the plane.

Sammie looked up at her mom. She could tell her mother was really scared. "Here, Mom, take my hand. Just relax and breathe deeply. You'll be just fine."

There were nice ladies in uniforms that were very pleasant and helpful. As they reached their seats, the lady asked Kate, "Who would like to sit by the window?"

"Not me!" cried Kate. "Let my daughter sit by the window."

"Hooray!" shouted Sammie.

"Mother, I can't believe you decided to forgive the O'Gradys so fast after all the years they avoided you."

"Sammie, holding grudges against people will only make you sad. Forgiving people, in the end, will give you peace. I want peace, and I think we'll find it, with the O'Grady's in Florida, I really do."

"Okay, Mom, I guess your right. I'll try and keep a good attitude toward them all."

There was still one aisle seat left. "I wonder if anyone will be seated here next to me?" commented Kate.

Just then, a lady with a suitcase came down the aisle and stopped at the open seat next to them.

"Oh, here's my seat. Hi, I'm Deborah Townsend." She put her suitcase in one of the upper storage places and sat down.

"Hello, I'm Kate, and this is my daughter, Sammie. We are going to Florida. Are you going to Florida too?"

"No, I'm going back home to Nashville, Tennessee. That's where I live. I was visiting my daughter in St. Cloud, Minnesota."

They then heard the pilot announce that the plane would be taking off in just a few minutes.

Mrs. Townsend looked at Kate, holding on to armrests really hard. "Are you all right, Kate?"

"No, I'm not all right. I'm really *scared*. It's my first flight, and I don't think I'm going to be comfortable during this fight at all."

Deborah just laughed, saying, "You'll be fine in just a few minutes after we've taken off. In a little while, you can get up and walk around. You're much safer in an airplane than you are in a car, and that's a fact!"

Deborah then pulled out a little tablet that had a lighted screen. Sammie then looked around the plane and saw others who had one of these things.

"Mrs. Townsend, what is that lighted thing you're holding? I've never seen one of those things before," inquired Sammie.

"Oh, my, you must have been living away from most towns and cities. It's my phone, Sammie. I can also watch movies on this, play games, and read any book I want."

Sammie wanted to be closer to Mrs. Townsend, "Mom, let's switch places. I want Mrs. Townsend to show me more about her phone."

"No, Sammie, I just couldn't sit next to the window. Let Mrs. Townsend sit next to the window, you sit in the middle, and I'll take the aisle seat."

Mrs. Townsend taught Sammie everything about her phone. She also let her play a lot of the games on her phone. Sammie was certainly mesmerized by her phone.

"Mother, I want to have one of these, please!"

Kate wanted to know how much one of these phones would cost, so she asked Mrs. Townsend about it.

"They are expensive. This one was over six hundred dollars," explained Mrs. Townsend.

"Wow, Sammie, we could never afford to buy one of these."

"I bet my grandfather would buy me one," she cried.

Soon the plane had arrived at the Nashville airport. They said their good-byes to Mrs. Townsend. She certainly had been a fascinating lady to talk to.

They had a layover in Nashville for about two hours. The airport was much bigger than the little one in St. Cloud. Sammie had lots of fun looking around at everything in the airport. After they had a nice dinner, they boarded the plane again.

"Mom, are you getting used to being on an airplane now?"

"Yes, Sammie, I am. I think I'll enjoy the rest of the trip now. Can I sit next to the window?"

"Yes, Mom, you may have my seat. I'm going to sleep for a little while."

Soon they were in the air flying to their final destination.

Chapter Six

Meeting New People

Back at the citrus ranch, Sadie and Samuel were discussing which rooms they would give Kate and Sammie in their mansion.

"Samuel, what would you think about me placing Sammie in Cody's old room? I could also place Kate is Davis's room."

"I guess it would be okay, Sadie, but please don't tell Kate that it was her husband's room or Sammie that it was her father's room unless they ask."

Simon, Sammie's uncle, was on his way to get Kate and Sammie at the Orlando Airport. Saturday was always a lot busier than the weekdays, but that's the day they choose to come. Amy asked if she could go with Simon to get them. Amy was the ranch foreman's daughter, who was ten.

Back on the plane, Kate and Sammie heard the pilot announce that they were preparing to land in Orlando. This time Kate was a little more comfortable and not as scared as the plane touched down. It was a very smooth landing.

As they left the plane and entered the terminal, they saw Simon. He greeted them with hugs.

"Oh, I brought along the ranch foreman's daughter. Her name is Amy Robinson."

"Hi, I hope you didn't mind me coming along with Simon, but I wanted to be the first to meet you!" cried Amy.

"I'm glad you came, Amy. I hope you'll show me around the big ranch," Sammie replied.

"I'd be more than happy to do that. Mrs. O'Grady, I hope you'll come with us while I'm showing Sammie the ranch."

"That sounds like fun, Amy. I'd love to come along with you both," responded Kate.

"Well, follow me," Simon commented, "and we'll go down and get your luggage, and then we'll be off to tour the O'Grady's Citrus Ranch."

As they reached the RV, Sammie smiled. The RV was bright orange, with the words printed on the side that said 'O'Grady's Citrus Ranch.' It also had pictures of oranges and grapefruit on the RV as well.

"Your RV sure is colorful, Simon," laughed Sammie. "It sure must be a good advertising tool for the citrus ranch."

"Yes, it is, and it works, Sammie," Simon laughed along with her.

Amy remarked, "I hope we can be best friends, Sammie. I'm ten, and they told me that you were eight, right?"

"Yes, that's right. I just turned eight."

"I've never had anyone to play with on the ranch except with my little five-year-old sister, Beverly, and my brother, Logan, who is fifteen.

"Uncle Simon, I bet my grandpa and grandma will be happy to have their only grandchild coming to live on their citrus ranch with them."

"Well, Sammie, they will, but soon my wife Hannah will be having our first baby. It's going to be a girl. We've already named her. Her name will be Kassie. She will be their second granddaughter."

"Maybe Amy and I can help Hannah with her new baby when it's born," cried Sammie.

"I'm sure Hannah will appreciate that. New mothers always need a helping hand."

Soon they were pulling up to a beautiful mansion.

"Wow, Uncle Simon, what a big house! I sure enjoyed the ride from the airport to the ranch. It took a while, but I loved seeing how beautiful Florida is," remarked Sammie.

"Yes," Kate also agreed. "Simon, I didn't have any idea that the ranch was so big."

Simon beeped the horn as they arrived at the mansion house. Amy got out, saying, "Hope to see you later, Sammie."

When they heard the horn, Samuel and Sadie came out. "How was your flight?" asked Sadie.

"It was the first time for both Sammie and me to fly in an airplane. It sure was a long flight, but I finally got used to it." Kate replied, smiling.

Samuel added, "Come on in. Let's get you both settled."

Simon and another man helped get their baggage into the mansion.

Sadie then said, "Follow me, Kate, and I'll take you and Sammie up to the rooms that will be all yours."

"Grandma, you didn't introduce that other man who helped Simon bring our bags into the mansion."

"Oh, you will be meeting him later, Sammie. He does lots of things around here, one thing he also does is being our butler."

Sammie then commented as she entered her new bedroom, "I love it, Grandma!"

"Make it your own, Sammie. Do whatever you want to do with it. We want you to feel right at home."

Sammie went and jump up on her new bed. She was beginning to think she might like living in Florida.

"Come this way, Kate," Sadie directed. "This will be your room. I hope you'll get to feel right at home with us very soon, my dear daughter-in-law. I know that you're going to want to be doing something with your time. Busy people are happy people. Don't you agree?"

"Yes, I do agree, Sadie. I'll do anything you'd like me, too," responded Kate.

"No, Kate, that's not what I exactly meant. I want you to do something that *you* love. You can help our cook, feed chickens on the farm, milk the cows, or come and join some of the clubs that I go to during the week. It doesn't matter except that you love what you pick and want to help."

"I'd love to help. Let me think about it, Sadie."

Shortly afterward, Sammie came into her mother's room. "I love your room, too, Mother. I sure can tell that my grandparents are prosperous."

"Sammie, let's go downstairs so that we can meet some of the others who we will be living with."

They first met the butler. "Hi, we're Kate and Sammie. We'll be living here now. Thanks for helping Simon with our luggage."

"I'm Joseph. We're all happy to have you here with us now. If there's anything that I can do to help you, please ask."

They then wandered into the kitchen. Amy was in there with a lady who looked like she was in charge. Amy hadn't left after all.

"Welcome to the 'O'Grady's Citrus Ranch. We're happy to have you here. I'm the cook here. My name is Maria."

Just then, a woman came in the back door of the kitchen. "Hello, Kate. I'm glad to see you again. I hope your flight was okay. I'm so glad everything is working out for you to be with us, and it's great to have more family here," explained Hannah, Simon's wife.

Sammie then added, "If I'm counting correctly, all of our family is here now on this beautiful ranch, right, Mom?"

Kate then added, "Yes, I believe your right, Sammie. We're so glad you have all invited us to be with you all now. Hannah, Simon tells us that your baby may be coming soon?"

"Yes, Kate. In just about six weeks. We're going to have a girl, and we've already named her Kassie," exclaimed Hannah.

"Yes, Simon told us on the way here. Hannah, I'm planning on being there for you," Kate replied.

Kate then suggested, "Sammie, let's go out for a short walk."

Amy tagged along. It was a perfect day. They then heard a motorbike approaching. The boy on the motorbike pulled right up to them.

"Hi, I'm Logan. My father is the ranch foreman. I see you've already met my sister, Amy."

"Nice to meet you, Logan," Kate remarked." I guess we'll be seeing you around."

"Yes, I'm sure you will. Bye, now." He looked back at Sammie and added, "Sammie, maybe I'll give you a ride on my motorcycle if your mom says it's okay." He then zipped off on his bike.

"Well, now, you've met my older brother. He's fifteen and goes to high school. I guess I'll be on my way home. See you later. We have school on Monday," cried Amy.

About thirty minutes later, Kate and Sammie decided to take a rest before dinner.

As they went up the stairs, Kate saw a housekeeper coming out of her room. "Hi, I'm Kate. I'll be sleeping in this room. What is your name?"

"I'm Justine. I was just checking to be sure everything was in order."

"Nice to meet you, Justine," expressed Kate. Justine then hurried away.

When Sammie entered her room, she was surprised to find one of the housekeepers dusting.

"Hi, I'm Sammie. I guess you're also one of the housekeepers. Everything looks wonderful. What is your name?"

"I'm Doris." She then hurried off.

Later that evening at dinner, Kate mentioned that they thought they had met almost everyone who lived on the ranch.

I don't believe you've met Letta, Melvin, and their little daughter Beverly yet. I'm sure that Amy must have told you about her parents. They live about a mile up that dirt road. They hire the pickers and run the small farm by their house," commented Sadie.

"Yes, you're right, Sadie. We haven't met them yet, but we will, right, Sammie?"

"Yes, I'm looking forward to that, Mom."

Chapter Seven

School

It was Sunday morning, and Sammie was up early. She went down to the kitchen. She found Maria making some pancakes.

"Mmm, I love pancakes! Could I have some? I'm starved, Maria," exclaimed Sammie.

"You sure can, would you like some bacon with that too?"

"Yes, that sounds wonderful! When do most of the rest of the family come down for their breakfast?"

"Well, it's Sunday, and everyone just comes down when they feel like it, but I've told them all that it better be before ten, or they'll have to fix their own," she smiled.

Just then, she saw Amy coming in the back door of the kitchen. "Maria, can I have some of what Sammie is having?"

"Yes, Amy, you know you're always welcome. You're just like one of the family. I've known Amy since she was just a baby," Marie laughed.

While the girls were eating, Amy expressed, "Tomorrow is school, Sammie. We have a bus that comes here at 8:15 a.m. to take us to school. Bob, our driver, always beeps his horn when he arrives. Our school is in Rockledge. A lot of the kids live in Rockledge, but there are also kids from all the outlying areas too that Bob brings to our school."

"Tomorrow, Amy, my grandmother, and my mom are taking me to your school to get me registered."

"I think you'll like our school. My teacher's name is Mr. Buford. I'm not sure who your teacher will be," Amy commented.

"Amy, where do you live since I know you don't live here at the mansion house?"

"Don't you remember? I told you before that we live down that dirt road about a mile." After they had finished their breakfast, Amy declared, "Now come with me, Sammie, and I'll show you where I live."

Both girls thanked Maria for their breakfast and ran out the back door of the kitchen.

"Here's the path or dirt road," Amy explained. "It will take about fifteen minutes to walk there."

As they got closer, Sammie shouted, "Oh, I see it now! It's a beautiful house!"

"Come on, let's go in. I'll introduce you to my mother. It's tough to catch Melvin, my father, at home. He's all over this ranch."

"I'd be pleased to meet your mother, Amy."

As they entered, Sammie saw Amy's mother, brushing a beautiful golden retriever.

"Mom, this is, Sammie."

"It's sure nice to meet you, Sammie. I'm Mrs. Robinson, but you may call me just Letta. My little five-year-old daughter, Beverly, is playing over in that corner, Sammie."

Sammie then went over and gave little five-year-old Beverly a big hug. "I'm going to be living in the big mansion house now. I hope to see more of you."

"Can I come and live with you in the big mansion house, Sammie?"

"No, Beverly, your mother, would miss you too much. I'll see you more, though, just by coming here once in a while."

"Come on, Sammie. I want to show you the farm that is just down the lane from our house."

Amy showed Sammie all over the farm. They had a big barn with three horses, four cows, two goats, seven pigs, and lots of chickens. Oh, and, of course, dogs and cats.

"This farm helps feed all of our full-time Mexican families. This big garden has many types of vegetables. They also have planted some other kinds of fruit trees so that they could have more choices of fruit to eat."

She continued, "They have a large underground cool place to store the foods that they can in glass jars. That helps the Mexican wives preserve the food for future use. They also have dairy cows so that they can have milk and all kinds of milk products. Your grandfather butches and freezes the meat from cows for all types of beef, pigs for pork, bacon, and ham, and, finally, they raise a lot of chickens."

"So, then they won't have to go to the food market, then will they, Amy?"

"Well, not for very much, Sammie, that's for sure. Some of the workers go fishing every so often so they can have fish too."

"We have about fifteen to twenty pickers who live here year-round," Amy further informed Sammie. "Some have their wives and children with them. They help keep the garden up, trim the trees, mend fences, and do lots of other odd jobs besides picking in harvest times. In the various peak picking seasons, your grandfather brings in guest pickers."

"Is that big long building over there to the north where they live?"

"Yes, come on, Sammie, and I'll show it to you."

"It's very nice. Can we go in and see it, Amy?"

"Yes, Sammie, follow me."

As they entered, several of the workers smiled and welcomed Amy. "Who is your friend, Amy?"

"This is Sammie. She's the granddaughter of Samuel and Sadie. She'll be living with them in the mansion house. Her mother will be living there too."

"Everything sure looks nice. My grandpa must value his pickers," cried Sammie.

"Yes, Sammie," remarked one the of workers. "Most of us have lived here for many years with our wives and children. During our harvest times and all through the year, many more pickers come to help get the various harvests in. We always treat these guest pickers with respect."

"Nice to have met you all. I hope to be able to see you again," Sammie responded.

Just as they were leaving, Amy's father drove up in his pickup. "Well, hello, Sammie. We finally get to meet each other. I'm always going this way and that."

Surprisingly, he gave her a big hug.

"I was wondering when I would meet you. Mr. Robinson."

"I hope you like living here on this big ranch." He then disappeared into the barracks.

The next morning they were all on their way to get Sammie registered for school. Sammie, Amy, and Amy's little sister, Beverly, were in the back seat being silly and noisy.

As they arrived, Amy jumped out of the car and yelled, "Follow me, Sammie, and I'll show you where the school office is." Sadie and Kate tried to keep up with the girls and finally did. Sadie took little Beverly to her kindergarten class.

After Sammie was registered, the principal, Mrs. Dillard, then took them all down to Mrs. Vaughn's third-grade class and introduced Sammie to the class. Her mother then hugged her, saying she would see her when she got home.

"Sammie, please take the seat next to Rebecca. Rebecca is in the third-row second seat. I hope you will enjoy being in our class. Please see me after school has ended. You'll need to have some homework to catch you up for the three weeks that you weren't here."

On the way back to the mansion, Kate spoke. "Sadie, I can't express how well you have treated us."

"I'm glad you decided to live with us," Sadie replied. She then asked, "Kate, have you decided yet what you'd like to do around the ranch?"

"Yes, Sadie. I'd love to help where ever I can. I mean, getting to know the ranch and its people, so that I can feel much more at home. I would like to help Maria in the kitchen and also help on the farm so I can get to know some of the full-time Mexican workers. I'll also want to help Hannah with her baby when it comes. Just a lot of things at first, then maybe I'll settle into something I want to do. I am pretty good at being an artist, but I haven't developed my talent there too much, but I would like to."

"I'm glad that you want to know the ranch and its people, Kate. You just let me know what and when you want to start."

After school, Amy and Beverly couldn't find Sammie. She saw Rebecca, and she told Amy that Mrs. Vaughn was giving Sammie some extra homework so she could catch up with the class.

"Oh, that's right! I do remember that now. Here she comes. Hurry Sammie, or we'll miss the bus!" cried Amy.

As they got on the bus, Bob, their bus driver, smiled and said, "I'd never leave any of you kids stranded here at school."

"Bob, this is Sammie, the new girl. She lives on the 'O'Grady Citrus Ranch' as Beverly, and I do."

"Welcome, Sammie. I guess we'll be seeing each other on the school days."

As they moved back on the bus to find a seat, a boy jumped up. "So, you're Sammie. I'm in your class. I'm Justin."

"It's nice to meet you, Justin."

Amy and Sammie saw a seat just ahead, but Justin grabbed Sammie and pulled her down in the seat next to him.

"Excuse me, but I'd decided that you're sitting with me." She tried getting up, but Justin pulled her back down.

Rebecca and Amy started shouting, "Justin, let her get up!"

Bob, the driver, pulled his bus over to the side of the road and then went back to where Justin and the girls where.

"Justin, this may be the last time you get to ride on my bus. You've had warning after warning. Now, let go of Sammie! You come up to the front of the bus right now. You'll be riding the rest of the way in the front seat of the bus to your destination."

Finally, the girls were dropped off at the ranch. Amy and Beverly ran their direction, and Sammie headed for the mansion house.

As she entered the mansion, her grandmother came and gave her a big hug. "How was your first day at school?"

"I have one more new friend. Her name is Rebecca. I liked her right away. We did have a little trouble with a boy on the bus, but Bob, the driver, put an end to it."

"What was this boy's name? It didn't happen to be Justin, did it, Sammie?"

"Yes, Grandma, that was his name, all right."

"I'll look into this, Sammie. I've had to do this once before."

"How did you hear about it the first time, Grandma?"

"I heard about it from Amy and some of her friends. They all have been bullied by him a little," she replied.

"So, Grandma, it still hasn't been solved then?"

"Apparently not, Sammie, but this time, it will be!"

Chapter Eight

Bullies

Mrs. O'Grady called the school principal, Mrs. Dillard, and told her all about Justin's latest bullying.

Mrs. Dillard then related to Mrs. O'Grady that Justin was on probation and that she had informed him that if he had one more problem that he would be given a lot of restrictions that he wouldn't like.

Justin and his parents were called into the principal's office the following morning. She handed his parents and Justin a paper stating the new restrictions he would have to follow for the next three months.

Justin looked at it and said, "This is too much! I won't be able to associate with any of my friends very much!"

Mrs. Dillard asked his parents, Mr. and Mrs. Martin, to read the restrictions out loud.

After reading them, she asked his parents, "Do you think I'm being too hard on your son with these restrictions?"

Mr. Martin spoke, "Not at all. We'll have some additional restrictions added to this for him at home as well."

His parents thanked the principal and left. Justin then ran down to his class.

When lunchtime came, Justin and his friend, Larry, walked down to the lunchroom together. Larry was also one of the school bullies as well.

"So, what restrictions did they place on you, Justin?"

"I have to ride in the front seat of the bus. At recess time, I'm allowed to bring a book but can't talk to any of the kids. At lunchtime, I have to sit by myself. It's not fair, Larry. I have to do this for three months!"

"Boy, I'm on probation right now too. I'd better be careful, or I might have even worse restrictions placed on me. I'd better tell Bobby and Caroline to watch their steps."

A few days later, Sammie made an appointment with Mrs. Dillard to talk about the bullies in their school. Amy went with her.

As they entered, Mrs. Dillard hugged Sammie and said how glad she was that she was a part of their school now.

"Mrs. Dillard, in my former school, we had some bullies too. After a program that the kids put together, just about all the bullies improve their behavior."

"Tell me what you did, Sammie, to have those kinds of results?"

"First, we put posters all over the school which the kids drew. They told the students in an assembly about calling 'B.' Kids would come running to help stop the bullie when any student would yell, "B." Within less than a month, there were very few problems."

"Thank you, girls. I think the restrictions we placed on Justin may scare the other bullies in backing off their bullying. We'll see what happens first, and if it continues, we'll look at some other things we can try."

Sammie and Amy told all the kids what they could about yelling "B" when anyone was bullying them. Pretty soon, all the kids in different classes knew about yelling "B." Sammie hoped that the principal wouldn't be upset with them not receiving her permission first.

It was just about a week later when Lois was walking home from school. Caroline caught up with her and exclaimed. "What is this talk about me and some of my friends bothering you kids?"

"Well, it's true, Caroline. You don't treat us girls very nice, and you say mean things about certain girls that aren't true. Now, may I go?"

"No, you may not!" She then pushed her down, yelling, "You'd better not be telling *anyone* that I'm saying bad things about my other classmates."

Lois then yelled, "B."

Two boys that were a little ahead of them heard someone calling "B," and came running. Another girl behind them also came running. Soon Joe and Adam were there, and Karlee was there just a few seconds later.

"Okay, Caroline, we have four witnesses of you being a bully. In the morning, we will be presenting what happened here to the principal," acknowledged Adam.

"You wouldn't dare do that!" she shouted.

"Watch us, Caroline," smiled Joe.

When the principal, Mrs. Dillard, received the four notes from the students about what happened after class, she called Caroline's parents in for a meeting the next morning.

Caroline's father spoke first after their introductions. "We know why she's here again. She's also in just as much trouble at home too."

The principle then handed one sheet to Caroline and one to her parents.

Caroline stood up. "You can't expect me to be this restricted!"

Her mother said, "I can think of some more things to add to this."

Her father then yelled, "Sit down, Caroline!"

After a little more conversation, Caroline left and went to her class.

Her parents then told the principle they just didn't know what to do with her.

Her father then added, "We will be taking her phone away for the three months. I hope this will help too." Her parents then left.

Caroline that night still had her phone. She called her friend Bobby. "Bobby, my parents are taking my phone away. I have even more restrictions than Justin does!"

"What could be worse? Do you have *all* of Justin's restrictions?" inquired Bobby.

"Yes, and more! I can't eat with anyone during lunch. I can't talk to anyone at recess and must be close to my teacher. I have to stay after school every day for an extra thirty minutes in my teacher's room."

Just then, her father came into her bedroom. "Say, good-bye, Caroline."

"I have to go, Bobby. See you at school tomorrow."

Her father then held out his hand. Caroline gave him her phone.

"We're taking your phone away for three months. If you continue to be a problem in our family, I will be adding a week to the three months. You may never get your phone back unless you start being a much better girl."

Somehow what happened to Caroline got all around the school.

Larry and Bobby were scared to step out of line. They were both on probation too.

It was about three weeks later, and there were almost no kids who stepped forward, saying they had been bullied.

Sammie was the most popular girl in their school. She had stopped almost all the bullying.

A few weeks had passed, and one late afternoon, there was some excitement on the ranch. Simon's wife, Hannah, called her husband on her cell. "Simon, come quickly. I think our baby is coming. Hurry!"

Simon was nearby. They then hurried to the hospital. They made in it time, and everything went well for Hannah. Simon and Hannah were now proud parents of their dear little Kassie.

Chapter Nine

Sammie's Birthday Party

Now that school was close to being finished, Sammie wondered what next year would be like. Would there still be bullies? Sammie would be soon going into the fourth grade at her school. Amy was leaving to go to middle school. How would she ever manage without her? She did have some comfort, though. She had made some terrific friends with Rebecca, Robin, and Jenifer. She, however, also did have Carissa, Rachel, and Deborah, as friends too.

Samuel, Sammie's grandfather, wanted Sammie to have a birthday party this year. She had adapted so well during a hard year, with losing her father and also making a significant change by moving to Florida, which would have been very hard for any eight-year-old. Samuel loved her so much and wanted her to be happy and, hopefully, to have the desire to stay on his ranch when she was older.

Samuel got Sammie's mother, Simon's wife, Hannah, and his wife, Sadie, to plan a wonderful party for Sammie. They wanted it to be before school had ended; that way, she could invite the girls she wanted to be at her party. They planned it for the last Friday and Saturday before school was to end.

Thursday, during the day, Sammie's special delivery presents arrived from her other grandparents who lived in London. This time there were three packages. Later that night, Sammie's grandparents from London called her, "Happy Birthday! We hope you'll enjoy your ninth birthday. Oh, and we hope you'll like the gifts that we sent."

"Thank you for loving me and keeping track of me. I hope you'll come to see me soon."

Friday evening finally came, and the girls started to arrive for her ninth birthday party. First, they had a fun evening making cookies. Next, the girls enjoyed a sleepover with lots of slumber games. In the morning, the girls all had a wonderful breakfast and played more games. Later in the morning, they went swimming. After lunch, they had some entertainment, with clowns and other fun things. Finally, the girls went horseback riding. It was a great party for Sammie, and her school friends sure had a ball too. Sammie thanked her mom, Hannah, and her grandma for making her ninth birthday so wonderful for her.

School was over for another year. The next Saturday morning, after everyone had had their breakfast, her grandfather came to her and expressed, "Sammie, I hope you enjoyed your birthday party with your friends."

"I did, Grandpa. It was the best birthday party I've *ever* had. Thank you so much for suggesting that I have this great birthday party. I've never had one that lasted two days before. I love you, Grandpa."

"How about you and I take a walk? I'd like to tell you some things about the ranch. You've been here on the ranch for about ten months now, and I think you don't know very much about the oranges and the grapefruits that we grow here on the citrus ranch. There are many different kinds of each."

"I didn't know that, Grandfather. I'd love to hear more about what goes on around the ranch."

"Come on, Sammie. Let's you and I ride over to the orange groves in my pickup."

When they got there, Sammie and her grandfather walked over to the trees in the orange groves, he pointed up, "Here is the most popular orange we grow. It's called a navel orange. We harvest it all through November to June, but the harvest times still could vary. Up a little further are the Valencia oranges. They are the next most popular orange we grow. We harvest them from March to October."

He continued, "There are about fifty varieties of oranges all through the world, Sammie."

"Wow, grandfather, that's a lot. How many varieties do you have here?"

"Just four right now, Sammie. We have two others, but not so many trees as the first two kinds that we've already discussed." They then drove a little further and got out of the pickup. "The other two are the Cara Cara oranges, which are harvested from December to May, and the Clementine orange. Their harvest time is much shorter. It's only in December and January."

"Grandfather O'Grady, can you tell me about the grapefruits now?"

"No, not today, Sammie. We'll save the rest for another day. I think you've learned a lot for this morning."

"Then, when can we do this again? I enjoy being with you, Grandfather."

"Well, maybe next week. How about this time next week? Then we'll talk about grapefruits and tangerines."

Another few days had passed. It was a sweltering summer day, and Sammie and Amy were walking through the mansion.

Sadie, Sammie's grandma, saw them and yelled, "Girls, would you come over here for a minute?"

"Why, yes, Grandma," Sammie replied.

"How would you like me to take you girls to 'Disney World' in a couple of weeks?"

"Yea! That would be great!" the girls shouted.

"Besides that, Sammie, I have another surprise announcement for you. How would you like Chloe to come with us? Your grandfather and I will pay for everything to get her here."

She continued, "All I've heard you talk about is your best friend since you've been here. I know you miss her. I also have listened to you and Chloe talking on the phone a lot, and I don't mind that at all, Sammie. Good friends are hard to find."

"Can we set a date, Grandma?"

"Yes, my dear, I'll give you a date by tomorrow when we can all go."

Sammie could hardly believe Chloe was coming! She couldn't wait to call her. How would Chloe take the news? Would she lay down on the floor and scream, or just scream?

The next morning at breakfast, Kate, Sammie, and her grandparents all ate breakfast together. Grandfather O'Grady spoke. "I hear you're going to 'Disney World' with Amy and one of your friends from Morris, Minnesota."

"Yes, Grandfather, but first, Grandma has to tell me the date."

Her grandmother then related, "Sammie, I have gotten a date. It will be on the 12th of June when I take you girls to Disney World, but Chloe will be here two days before that. I didn't want it to be too close to any holidays when so many people are there."

"Great! I'll call Chloe after breakfast."

"Oh, and Sammie," added her grandfather, "I can get special executive tickets, so when there are these huge long lines, you'll just get in the executive line and go through much faster. That way, you can see so much more of the park in one day."

"Really, Grandfather, I didn't know there was such a thing! That will make Chloe happy, not having to wait in those long hot lines, just to have fun. Sometimes that doesn't make good sense to me," she laughed.

Smiling, he added, "It sure doesn't make sense to me either, Sammie, but kids are tough and don't seem to mind it when they're happy and having fun."

Chapter Ten

Sammie Learns O'Grady's Family History

When Sammie had finished her breakfast, she excused herself and ran to the library phone to call her friend, Chloe. She was so excited to tell her the news. When she called, Chloe answered.

"Hi, Chloe, I can't believe you answered. I have some exciting news for you!"

"Are you finally going to come for a visit, Sammie?" she yelled.

"No, it's *much better* news than that, Chloe! You'll be coming here on June 10th two days before we take you to *'Disney World,'* here in Orlando, Florida. My grandmother, Sophie, will be taking us. I'll be bringing along my friend, Amy. Her family lives and works here on the ranch. Her father is the ranch foreman, so he is in charge of everything here on the ranch. They have a beautiful home of their own, by a big farm, which is part of the ranch also."

Chloe screamed, just like Sammie thought she would. "I can't believe anything like this would *ever, ever* happen to me. It's just almost impossible to think about Sammie!"

"Well, believe it, Chloe, you're coming, and I'll be so glad to see you in person. I love you and have missed you so much. I'm so pleased that my grandmother lets me call you so much."

"Well, Sammie, it's only about two weeks from now, and we will be together. Thank your grandfather and grandmother for inviting me. Now I'm going to run out and tell everybody I know that I'm going to 'Disney World' in about two weeks. I'll be talking to you soon. Bye now."

It was the next Saturday, and time for Sammie and her grandfather to get together for another walk. This time they had to take grandpa's pickup again because all of the grapefruit and tangerine trees were on the other side of the vast ranch.

They finally arrived on the far side of the ranch. "Well, this is where we grow the grapefruits, Sammie."

They got out of the truck. "The grapefruit that grows on these trees are called flame grapefruit. There are mainly two kinds of grapefruit. The red grapefruit is, is very popular, and the white grapefruit is almost as popular as the red. They harvest these from November to April, so they have a very long harvest time."

They then drove down a little further, "Here are the tangerine trees. There are two different kinds. The first is the Fallglo Tangerine, which harvests in November and, finally, the Dancy Tangerine, which harvests in December. That's about it, Sammie."

"I think everything here on the ranch is wonderful, Grandfather!"

"Sammie, I know you're only nine years old. I want you always to remember that you're a true O'Grady. Your real natural father was Cody O'Grady. I hope you'll always love the ranch as I do, and will *want* to stay so that the O'Gradys will always have control of this ranch."

"I will, Grandfather!"

Her grandfather continued, "I'm getting older, Sammie, and your Uncle Simon will be taking over the ranch when I can't do it any longer. I hope that will still be a ways off. As you graduate from high school, you'll want to leave for college. When you finish, I hope you'll come back and help Hannah and Simon run the ranch. I'll be putting you in my will as a part-owner in remembrance of my son Cody. Your mother will also be in the will; this will be in remembrance of my son, Davis. Of course, Simon will be the third person named in my will. Each of you will have a one-third interest in my ranch when I pass."

"Really, Grandpa, you're going to include *me* in your will! Thank you so much."

"Yes, again, you are an O'Grady! Sammie, always remember that. We hope that Hannah will have some more kids besides little Kassie."

"Are we finished now?" she asked him.

"No, Sammie. I thought maybe you'd like to go horseback riding with me now."

"Yes, I would love to, Grandfather!" she shouted.

As they reached the stables, Samuel saw his stableman out in front. He beeped his horn.

He came over to the car. "Lester, we're here to go riding. Would you saddle up my horse and get Sally, you know the one that Sammie likes to ride."

"Yes, I'd be happy to, Mr. O'Grady. It's always great to see you, Sammie. I hope you'll continue to love living on this beautiful ranch as much as I do."

"Lester and his helpers take very good care of the horses. He also takes care of a small herd of cattle as well. We have other employees who use the horses too."

Soon, Lester had the horses ready, and off they went. It was the most beautiful morning for riding. Sammie loved getting to know her grandfather even better.

Later that evening, she found her grandfather in his den. She entered, "Grandfather, can I talk with you for a minute?"

"Why, certainly, Sammie. Do come in and sit down."

"Grandfather, how did the 'O'Grady's Ranch' get started? Were you the founder of this beautiful place?"

"That's an excellent question, Sammie. I am so glad you asked. Sit down here next to me."

"What year was it that the ranch started?" she inquired.

"First, it wasn't me that put together this ranch. It was my father, Clifford O'Grady, your great grandfather. He started it in 1921. America was doing great, and everyone was making a lot of money in the stock market. Sammie, do you know what a stock market is?"

"No, not for sure," she responded, looking a little confused.

"Well, if you own a stock, you own part of some company. Your great grandfather made a lot of money owning these stocks, but he decided he didn't trust the stock market to keep going up as fast as it was. He then decided to look for something he could buy. So in searching, he found a large tract of land in Florida. No one was buying much of anything in Florida during those early years."

"Didn't people like Florida?"

"Not many people lived here, Sammie. The land was swampy in certain places, and the people who did live here had been here for many years, and they lived in pretty poor conditions."

"So, why would my great grandfather want to buy land in Florida then?"

"He knew things were changing fast, and he could see how he could make a lot of money selling oranges. There were lots of people available to hire when he would need them."

"When did he start planting the trees?"

"I believe it was about the third year after he purchased the land. Your great grandfather did get the men he needed to put together this wonderful ranch. He got a lot of contracts with stores and other big wholesalers to sell his oranges, and then he started making a lot of money."

"Then everything was going great then?"

"Well, yes, and no. There were no roads, electricity, phone lines, or water to the property. So it took a while to get that done. By 1929 things were still booming in the stock market. Then one day, the market crashed, and most all the rich people's money just vanished. Many of those rich people were very sad. Some even jumped out of windows because they couldn't handle losing most everything they had."

"Did my great grandfather lose his fortune too?"

"No, Sammie. He had paid for everything that he had bought. No one could take anything away from him. He kept getting richer and richer. I was his only son, so I inherited the whole ranch when he passed away. I love this ranch, and I hope you will too."

"Thanks for telling me all of this, Grandfather." She then left after giving him a big hug.

It was now the 10th of June. Joseph, who was their chauffeur, along with being the butler, took Sammie and her mom to the airport to get Chloe.

Chloe sure looked happy when they met her at the airport. They hugged each other over and over again. It had been so long since they had seen each other. "Come on, Chloe, let's go down and get your luggage, and then Joseph will take us to the ranch," stated Sammie's mother.

"Joseph, this is my friend, Chloe, as you've heard me talk about so often. Chloe, this is Joseph. He does lots of things around the ranch, and is a long term employee."

Soon they reached the ranch. There were a few employees to greet Chloe. Amy had brought her little sister, Beverly. She had the cutest dimples.

Sammie began introducing Chloe all around the mansion. "Chloe, you'll be sleeping with me in my bedroom. I have a huge bed."

Chloe followed Sammie up to her room. "Wow, Sammie, your bed *is* big. I'd sure like to have a bedroom like this one!"

"I sure was surprised when my grandmother offered me such a wonderful bedroom to be in!" replied Sammie.

Chapter Eleven

Disney World

As Chloe had dinner that first night with the O'Grady's, she was starting to enjoy being there. That evening, Amy came over to watch some TV with Chloe and Sammie. Finally, it was time to head for bed.

Amy remarked as she was leaving, "Nice to have met you, Chloe. Even though I've been to Disney World before, I always love going. I sure am excited to be going again with you both."

Before going to bed, Sammie gave her grandparents and her mother hugs. As they both went up to Sammie's bedroom, Chloe declared, "I can't believe how big your bed is!"

In the morning, Sammie shouted, "Tomorrow, we're going to Disney World!"

After their breakfast, Sammie asked, "Chloe, have you ever ridden a horse before?"

"No, I haven't," she responded.

"Well, that's what we're going to do this morning!" cried Sammie.

As they arrived at the stables, Lester saw them coming. "So, this is your friend that came from Morris, Minnesota. Welcome, Chloe! I guess you're here to do some riding."

"Lester, I've never been on a horse before. Can you give me a real gentle horse?" Chloe inquired.

"Why, yes. I have just the right horse for you."

"Lester, would it be too much to ask for you to come with us? I'm not experienced enough in case something was to go wrong, and this being Chloe's first time riding, I'd feel better having you along."

"You girls caught me at just the right time. I'd be more than happy to come with you both."

The girls had a great time with Lester. Chloe enjoyed learning how to ride a horse and seeing the ranch. They were both getting so excited about going to Disney in the morning.

A little later that afternoon, Chloe exclaimed, "I don't know if I can sleep tonight or not, Sammie! I was just thinking about going to Disney World tomorrow, and then there was the flight here. It is almost more than I can take in."

"Were you scared of being on the airplane, Chloe?"

"A little at first, but the flight was so long that I got used to it after a while. I began to think we'd never get here."

That afternoon it was hot, so the girls went swimming. "Sammie, you sure are lucky to have this big swimming pool!"

After their swim, they both played in Sammie's bedroom until dinner time.

Just before dinner, Kate, Sammie's mother, handed her some information about all the things that they would see the next day with Sadie, Sammie's grandmother.

"Look, Chloe, it says here that there are 46 different rides we can choose from and *four* theme parks!"

Chloe then took the brochure and commented, "I want to go to Space Mountain and the Magic Kingdom where Cinderella's Castle is. Look, Sammie, the Animal Kingdom!"

After dinner, they watched some TV with the family and finally headed for bed. That night neither of the girls slept very well.

They were up at 7:00 a.m. Sammie knew that in an hour, they would be leaving. The girls wanted to arrive at Disney World by 9:00 a.m.

It was 8:00 a.m., and Joseph was out in front with their limousine. They were on their way and soon arrived at Disney World. The girls could hardly contain themselves.

They had a whole day to see as much as possible. First, they went to Space Mountain, then to the Magic Kingdom. They also enjoyed seeing Cinderella's Castle and so many other things in Fantasyland. It seemed like all the girls were doing was eating. Lunchtime came, and they all had a varied selection of foods. Every time they saw some goodies, Sadie let them have them.

After lunch, they saw the Coral Reefs. They spent some time there. They loved seeing so much sea life. When they left, Chloe saw a big carousel or the merry go round.

"I've *never* been on a carousel. Let's go! I want to ride on it!" Chloe shouted.

They all rode the carousel three times, each time picking a different animal to ride on. Chloe was having the time of her life. Amy and Sammie were enjoying the day as well.

As the afternoon drew on, they got to drive cars on the speedway. The last thing they wanted to do was to go to Epcot, which Sadie told them they would love. On the way there, Chloe started holding her stomach.

"Sadie, I am not feeling well." She then ran over to one of the benches and doubled over crying. The Disney Clinic was nearby. A worker saw her and quickly got a wheelchair, and took her to the clinic.

One of the doctors looked her over and smiled and told Sadie that this was a common occurrence. "Just let her rest here for a little while. I've given her something to settle her stomach."

Chloe cried, "I've ruined the whole day. I hope you'll all forgive me."

Sadie added, "The doctors told me that this happens to a lot of kids, Chloe. You're going to be here for two weeks. We'll plan to come back here one more time. Next time we'll be more careful that you don't eat too many goodies, Chloe."

The girls all hollered, "Yea."

Soon they were home. Chloe went up to Sammie's room and took some more medicine, trying to get over her sick stomach.

That evening she ate just a little, but by morning she was just fine. Sammie's mother loved riding the horses and suggested that that's what they should all do. They all then headed for the stables.

"I loved riding with you the other day, Sammie. I am so glad that we get to go again," Chloe related.

When they got there, they found Amy was there helping Lester around the stables with various things.

"Hi, Amy!" declared Sammie.

"I'm helping Lester clean out some of the horse stalls," Amy smiled. "I see that you all came to ride this morning.

I'd go with you, but I need to finish cleaning out eight more stalls."

"Well, hello again, Chloe," stated Lester. How are you enjoying Florida?"

"We went to Disney yesterday, as you know, and we had a wonderful time until I got sick, that is."

Lester then asked Amy, "Would you get Sally saddled up for Chloe, and I'll get Sammie's and Kate's horses ready."

Kate then added, "Lester, I'd be happy to come to help you around the stables. I've been going all over the ranch, helping here and there, getting to know a lot of the people who work here."

"That would be fine, Kate. One of the things which needs additional attention is exercising the horses more. It's hard to keep up with it all by myself. I'd be happy to have you go with me."

"That sounds like *fun*, Lester, not work," she laughed.

Chloe had ten days left before she would be returning home. Sadie and Kate were trying to keep Chloe and Sammie busy with seeing a lot of things that Florida had to offer.

Just three days later, Kate took the girls to Disney World instead of Sadie. This time she made sure the girls weren't overeating.

Disney World was just as enjoyable as the first time. The girls went to the Coral Reefs, Discovery Land, the Haunted Mansion, and finally saw some of Epcot. It was a great day for them all.

The last few days Chloe was there they took her to the Crayola Experience, Boggy Creek Air Boat Rides, and to see another aquarium, which was even much bigger than the one at Disney.

It was finally time to take Chloe to the airport. She then admitted, "I was getting a little homesick, Sammie. I've never been away from home this long before. I'm so glad that your grandmother let me call home so often."

She was finally gone. Sammie was so glad that Chloe had such a good time, and hoped that maybe someday she could go to visit her in Morris, Minnesota.

Chapter Twelve

The Mall

There was still a lot of summer left. Sammie wondered how she would be spending the rest of it. Her good friend from school, Rebecca, only lived about three miles down the country road from them.

One Friday morning, Sammie called Rebecca, "Rebecca, would you like to go with my grandma and me to the 'Millennia Mall' in Orlando?"

"Yes, I would love to. It's a huge mall, Sammie. I know you'll love it. What time would we be going?"

"About eleven, that way we could eat lunch in the mall and have the afternoon to see everything. Go and check with your mother and call me back."

"She's right here, Sammie." She asked her mother and then reported, "It's okay, I'll see you at eleven."

Joseph, their chauffeur, was out in front of the mansion waiting for Sadie and Sammie. Once they were in the limousine, Joseph headed for Rebecca's.

They all soon arrived in Orlando. Sadie always loved going to the Millennia Mall and was happy this time to have Sammie and Rebecca with her.

As Sadie got out of the limousine, she told Joseph, "We should finish around 3:30 p.m., so stay close around the entrance about that time. I'll call you when we're ready to leave."

Sammie had been to some of the other malls, but nothing this big before. After a nice lunch, they shopped all afternoon. Around 4:00 p.m., Sammie's grandmother told the girls, "I need to find a place to sit. I'm feeling a little faint."

A couple that was nearby saw this lady heading for a bench. "Ted, I know that lady. She's Mrs. O'Grady. They own that huge citrus ranch. They're very wealthy."

They drew nearer so they could hear them taking. Sammie exclaimed, "Grandma, I'll go and get some help at the mall office. I'll be right back. Rebecca, you stay here with my grandmother."

Rebecca shouted, "Not that way, Sammie! It's the other way."

Doris then said to Ted. "We have an opportunity here. We're going to kidnap that little granddaughter of Mrs. O'Grady."

They began to follow Sammie. Doris shouted out, "Little girl, we heard you talking to your grandmother. There's a clinic this way. Follow us! We'll show you the way."

"Oh, thank you. You're so very kind."

Then as they got next to her, Ted pulled out a knife and said, "Keep walking and don't yell out, or I *will* hurt you. Do you understand, little girl?"

"Yes, I do, and my name is Sammie. Why are you doing this?"

"Never mind, Sammie, just keep walking, and don't make any foolish moves," cried Doris.

Soon they were outside. "Doris, we couldn't have been any luckier! Our car is just down the block." They all then got into their station wagon. Ted got behind the wheel, and Doris sat in the back with Sammie.

Just then, Joseph, Sadie's chauffeur, was driving by in the O'Grady's limousine, and he saw Sammie being pushed into this green station wagon. Sadie hadn't called for him to come and get them, so he decided to follow them.

As Ted drove away from the mall, Joseph followed them. They hadn't gone very far when he saw them stop in front of a house. Joseph watched as the lady pulled Sammie out of their car, and they all walked into this house of theirs. He then drove by the house, writing down the address, and then he phoned the police.

Back in the mall, Sadie was getting worried because Sammie had not returned. She then called a security man that was walking past them. He called the clinic and talked to some people there. No one had seen a little girl named Sammie.

Just then, Sadie got a phone call from Joseph telling her all about Sammie's kidnapping and that he just happened to be passing by the mall and saw this couple taking Sammie and pushing her into their station wagon. He then related that he followed the kidnappers to their house, which happened to be only a short distance from the mall, and finally told her that he had notified the police as to where she was.

Sadie then told Joseph all about her feeling faint and that she had sent Sammie for someone to come to help her.

Now Sadie understood why Sammie had not come back.

"I am feeling better now, Joseph. We'll meet you at the main entrance of the mall in a few minutes."

Joseph soon picked them up and headed over to the address where the couple lived who had kidnapped Sammie. They parked just a few houses away.

Joseph had told the police that it was Mrs. O'Grady's granddaughter. When the police were arriving, they saw the limousine near the address. The police car then stopped right next to them. One of the officers got out of his car and came up to the window of the limousine. "Mrs. O'Grady, we are here to get your granddaughter back."

"What are your plans for getting her back, officer?"

"There's a special group of officers coming that know just how to handle this kind of thing. I think this couple will let your granddaughter go when they see what they're up against."

"But, officer, what if they *don't*?"

"We'll just have to wait and see, Mrs. O'Grady."

Inside the house, Doris ordered Sammie, "You go over there and sit in the big chair in the corner."

"You better let me go!" cried Sammie.

"Not on your life, Sammie! You're worth about a million dollars, and your grandfather will pay us!"

"Ted, go and find some rope. We'd better tie her to this chair. We don't want her running off."

Just then, Ted looked out their front window. "Doris, there's a bunch of police cars out in front of our house!"

"How can that be? That's impossible. How could they have found out that we kidnapped her in this short of time?"

Soon there were even more police cars that came. An officer with a loud bull horn spoke. "We know you have kidnapped Sammie O'Grady. If you let her go, things will go much easier for you."

Inside the house, Ted asked, "Doris, what shall we do?"

"You'd better let me go!" cried Sammie. "You heard what the police officer said!"

"She's right, Doris. We have no other choice," cried Ted.

"Okay, Sammie," acknowledged Doris. "Carefully open the front door and go out."

Sammie opened the door and stepped out, and then seeing her grandma, ran to her.

"How did you ever find me so fast?"

Her grandmother then explained, "It was surely a miracle that Joseph just happened to be passing by when you were being kidnapped."

Doris and Ted then surrendered and were taken into custody.

As Sammie and her grandmother got into their limousine, the police captain came up to them and exclaimed, "It was a miracle that your granddaughter was rescued so fast, Mrs. O'Grady. Someone up there must have been looking over her."

On the way home, Sadie had called her husband and filled him in on everything that had happened. It all happened so fast that the newspapers and TV stations didn't hear about it until it was over.

Rebecca hugged Sammie on the way back. "We were worried when you didn't come back with help for your grandmother. We then heard from Joseph that you had been kidnapped, which was almost too hard to believe!"

"If I didn't believe in miracles before, I sure do now," cried Sammie.

When they arrived back at the mansion, it seemed like almost everyone was waiting for them. Sammie sure got a lot of hugs.

Chapter Thirteen

The Surprise Phone Call

It was July, and it was so hot and muggy. Sammie was not used to this at all. She was sure glad for air-conditioning. They had just finished the harvest of the navel oranges in June. Her grandfather told her that the harvest was very good this year.

They were also harvesting the Valencia oranges now as well, and would until October.

Sammie and Amy were always involved with all the harvests. With summer in full swing, they would help in the early morning hours and sometimes later after their dinner.

When school was in session, they helped most days after they got home from school from about 4:00 p.m. to 6:00 p.m. After dinner, the girls were free to do the homework that they had received from the school.

Sammie was so thankful for having such a large swimming pool. She swam almost every day during the summer.

It was the first part of July and Maria, their cook, had just finished making Sammie a nice lunch. She was hungry from working in the groves that morning. "What are your plans for the afternoon, Sammie?"

"I don't have any, Maria. I'm tired. I may take a nap," she smiled.

Just then, Amy came in the back door of the kitchen. "Anything left, Marie?" she asked.

"Yes, Amy, I have some nice hot soup left."

"You're kidding, of course. Not on a *hot* day like this!" she laughed.

"Then, I'll make you a ham and cheese sandwich. I also have some chips to go with your sandwich. Earlier this morning, I made some cookies which you girls may have as well."

"Sammie, my father gave me the rest of the day off. Let's do something fun!" exclaimed Amy.

"You mean your father expected you to work on this hot day? And besides, Amy, what is there to do anyway on a day this hot?"

Just then, her grandfather came into the kitchen. "How would you girls like to go swimming with me right now?"

They both screamed, "Yes, we would!" "I'll go up and get my swimming suit, Grandfather."

"Mr. O'Grady, we'll have to stop by my house to get my swimming suit."

"Amy, I have a swimsuit that may fit you. Come up to my bedroom," cried Sammie. They did find a swimsuit that did fit her. Sammie's mother had brought a few swimsuits that were a little larger, with Sammie growing so fast.

The big swimming pool they had on the ranch was used often, but to have Sammie's grandfather offer to take the afternoon off and to go swimming with them on this hot day was a real treat for the girls.

Sammie's mother was enjoying doing all sorts of things around the ranch and feeling more at home after these last few months of being there. She especially enjoyed working with Lester around the stables. They were having a lot of fun exercising the horses almost every day. Kate was starting to like Lester and wondered if that could be a problem with Lester's boss, Mr. O'Grady.

After the girls got home from swimming, Sammie was tired and wanted to take a rest. It was about 4:00 p.m. when she entered the mansion. She then heard the phone ringing. One of the housekeepers, Justine, answered it. She then called out to Sammie, who was just going up the stairs. "Miss Sammie, the phone's for you."

"Thank you, Justine. Hello," she said when she reached the phone.

"Hi, Sammie, this is Cami."

"It's so nice to hear from you, Cami. How are your sisters, Lexie and Jennifer?"

"Everyone here is doing great! I'm calling to tell you that we are coming to Florida this next Wednesday to go to Disney World. Chloe told us how great it was, and then we girls all begged our mother to take us. To our surprise, she agreed."

"I can hardly wait to see you all," remarked Sammie. "Of course, you'll stay with us here at the citrus ranch."

"No, Sammie. Our mom has made reservations at the Disney World Hotel Resort for us. We are planning on staying for five days. Our mom said she would be taking us to see other things as well."

"I hope you'll be coming out to the ranch before you go back."

"Yes, of course, you silly, we will plan on coming out there, Sammie. And there is another surprise. My mother has booked a room for you and your mother so you both can be with us while we are here. You'll get to do all the things that we are going to do!"

"I hope my mother will think it's okay that your mother is renting rooms for us at the Disney World Hotel Resort. I think she will. I'm so excited to see you all. I can hardly wait for Wednesday to come," cried Sammie.

Kate, Sammie's mother, did agree to be with Kathy and her girls for the five days. She could hardly wait to see how much the triplets had grown and changed.

Kate made arrangements with Joseph to pick up Kathy and her girls at the airport and take all of them to their hotel at Disney World. It was so nice of Kathy to have made these hotel reservations for Sammie and her mother. Sadie, Sammie's grandmother, was always so good about letting Kate use Joseph, her chauffeur, for special occasions like these.

As they arrived at the airport and were waiting for them to exit the plane, they finally saw Kathy, the girl's mother, and her daughters, Cami, Lexie, and Jennifer coming off the plane.

All the triplets rushed to Kate. They were now eight years old.

"Katie," cried Jennifer, "I'm so glad you'll be with us during our stay here."

"Kate, I hope I didn't offend you by renting rooms at Disney for you and Sammie, but we wanted to be with you as much as possible. The girls and I are looking forward to going out to the citrus ranch on our last day to see where you now live. I hear that it's pretty nice," commented Kathy, the triplets' mother.

Two days were filled with Disney World and then other exciting things that Kate had suggested to them. On the fifth day, they spent the whole day on the ranch. Sammie took the triplets into the various citrus groves and told them all about the different kinds that they grew there.

The triplets got to meet Rebecca, one of Sammie's best friends. All the girls played together until their mother called them, saying, "Cami, Lexie, Jennifer, it's time to go now."

Finally, Joseph took Kathy and her girls back to their hotel. The hotel had a shuttle bus that would take them to the airport the next morning. Sammie and her friend Rebecca went with them back to their hotel to say their final good-byes. There were lots of hugs as they departed.

On the way back, Rebecca commented, "It sure must have been very different for you living in a little town like Morris, Minnesota."

"It wasn't that bad living in a little town, Rebecca. We had all the things a big city has, except for all the tons of people, houses, buildings, cars, buses, and trucks."

"What about the nice malls and big supermarkets?"

"If we wanted those things, we were only about an hour and a half from St. Cloud, Minnesota."

"Well, maybe it wouldn't be *too* bad living there, after all, Sammie," laughed Rebecca.

Chapter Fourteen

A New Classmate

Time was going too fast for Sammie. Two more years passed, and Amy was a teenager at thirteen and would be entering high school in just one year. Sammie was eleven and was entering middle school. She was happy that she would be in middle school at least one year with Amy.

Sammie was beginning to be a regular helper with Amy, harvesting the oranges and grapefruit after school and on some weekends. Sammie knew that she would most likely be running the ranch with her Uncle Simon in the future. Simon and Sammie had always gotten along very well, and she also liked his wife, Hannah, and their dear little Kassie.

It was sad for Sammie as she started middle school. Three of her friends, Robin, Carissa and, Deborah, had all moved away. She was glad to still have Rachel, Jennifer, and Rebecca as her friends.

Bob was still the bus driver who took kids to their elementary and middle schools. Sammie wondered how Amy was going to get to high school next year. The high school was in Melbourne. There was a bus, but it took too long to get there, and the times weren't right to catch the bus anyway.

It was the first day of school. When Bob stopped to get Rebecca, she got on the bus as usual. As she was entering, she saw a new boy sitting about halfway back on the bus. She squealed as she approached the boy.

"Are you Lucas Bowen?" she inquired excitedly.

"Yes, I am. I'll be going to your middle school."

"What's your name?" Lucas inquired of her.

"I'm Rebecca."

"Why is a singing star like you going to just a regular school like ours?"

"My parents just bought a little ranch with some animals on it. It's always been their dream. Since I make a lot of money, they used some of it to buy this ranch."

"What about your singing around the country?"

"My parents only let me book things on a Saturday or a Sunday so that I can get back to school on Mondays."

"May I sit next to you, Lucas?"

"Yes, please do, Rebecca. Maybe when we get to your school, you could be my guide and introduce me to some of the kids."

"I'd love to, Lucas!" cried Rebecca.

Just then, the bus stopped, and Sammie, Amy, and Beverly got aboard. They saw Lucas and Rebecca sitting together.

Amy and Sammie ran down the aisle. "You're Lucas Bowen, aren't you?" Sammie almost shouted.

"Yes, I am, and as I told your friend, Rebecca, I'll be going to your school. I'll let her tell you the rest of my story later, okay?"

As other kids got on the bus, the same thing happened over and over. The kids were asking Lucas lots of questions. Lucas was trying to be polite to the kids and hoped they would soon be arriving at the school, which they finally did. His new teacher knew he was coming and would meet him when the bus arrived. She was there to rescue him.

"Hello, Lucas! I'm Miss Hogan. Please follow me."

He gladly followed her. Miss Hogan took him into the gym, where the principal was having all the students assemble.

After everyone was in the gym, the principal had Lucas stand. The principal then addressed the students. "Students, this is Lucas Bowen. He will be attending our school. I think most of you know Lucas Bowen. He's a very popular singer. *Please,* treat Lucas as just one of the students. I know this will be hard. Just smile and say hi. Lucas can't possibly talk to everyone about his life. Anyone bothering Lucas could be suspended."

He continued, "We are looking forward to the new school year. You may now all return to your classes."

When Lucas got to Miss Hogan's class, she asked him to pick where he would be most comfortable. He decided to sit next to Rebecca.

At lunchtime, the teacher reminded her students about not bothering Lucas. Most of the kids were kind and didn't bother him. Rebecca made sure that she reminded the kids that they could be suspended if they bothered Lucas.

Rebecca showed Lucas to the lunchroom. He, of course, sat with Rebecca, and she invited some of her friends to sit with them. Sammie was so happy to be one of them.

It was quite a day for Lucas. He was so thankful for Rebecca. As they got on the bus to go home and were both seated, Lucas addressed Rebecca. "Would you like to have dinner with my family and me tonight? You've been my lifesaver today, and I want to thank you. Please say yes, Rebecca."

"Yes, I'll call my mother and tell her all about what's been going on today. I don't know whether she'll believe me," she laughed.

All the kids on the bus heard what Lucas said and passed it around. Sammie was jealous of her friend but tried not to show it. Sammie, Amy, and Beverly's stop came, and they said their good-byes.

After calling her mother on her cell phone, Rebecca was so glad that her mother had given her permission to go to have dinner at Lucas's home. His parents told Rebecca about how Lucas had become famous. She was beginning to like Lucas.

After about a week, things at school were mostly returning to normal. Lucas was staying close to Rebecca. Everyone was starting to think Lucas was beginning to like Rebecca.

Sammie was missing Rebecca, now that she was with Lucas most of the time. She began to spend more time with her other friends.

One morning a few days later, Sammie was waiting for the bus with Amy and Beverly. Bob, their bus driver, soon arrived. As they boarded, Sammie noticed that Lucas was sitting alone. She wondered if Rebecca was sick. She'd wanted to get a little more acquainted with Lucas. She stopped at where he was sitting. "May I sit with you, Lucas?"

"Yes, you're Sammie, aren't you? I've had lunch with you and your friends. You were always so quiet at the lunch table. Rebecca has told me a little about you. You're the rich girl. Your family owns that big citrus ranch, right?"

"Yes, Lucas, my family does. You know, Lucas, Rebecca is my best friend, and since you've come, she sure spends a lot of time with you. I miss her."

"Well, Sammie, I'm joining the basketball team. Some of boys from our school came out to our little ranch and invited me to join their team. I think they're great guys, and I'll be spending more time with them now that I'm getting to know so many more kids."

"Lucas, I know you'll still be good friends with Rebecca, and I hope with me too."

"Yes, Sammie, I will. I shouldn't say this, but I hope you and I could be better friends too," he smiled.

Sammie couldn't believe he said that. She decided *not* to tell Rebecca what he said, though.

Chapter Fifteen

The Puppy

The fall season was here, and the harvesting of the navel and Valencia oranges was almost over. The weather was cooling a little in October. Everyone was happy about that.

One afternoon as Amy, Beverly, Rebecca, and Sammie were on their way home on the bus, they heard Lucas and his buddies laughing about something. Sammie was so happy that she and Rebecca could spend more time together now and that Lucas had found some male friends.

When their bus stopped at the citrus ranch, Amy, Beverly, and Sammie got off. As the bus pulled away, they heard a speeding car approaching. As the car got closer to them, someone in the vehicle threw something out their window.

Sammie shouted, "Amy, they threw a puppy out their window!"

They both ran to see where the puppy had landed. There was a lot of tall grass on the sides of the highway. Both Amy and Sammie looked and looked.

"I can't see the puppy anywhere, Amy."

"Sammie, we *have* to find the puppy before we can leave!"

Beverly was too afraid to look for the puppy because she thought it might be dead.

Suddenly, both girls heard the puppy whining. They followed the sound.

"I *see* the puppy, Amy!" shouted Sammie.

"Oh, Sammie, he's hurt!" exclaimed Amy.

Sammie carefully picked the puppy up. It was still whining.

"Amy, I'm going to take the puppy to the mansion, and I'll call a vet to come."

"Let me know what the vet says, after he leaves, okay, Sammie?"

"Okay, Amy, I will call you."

Then Amy remarked, wondering, "Sammie, what if the vet wants to take the puppy back to his clinic?"

"I'll make sure to tell him that I want to keep the puppy, and I will help nurse him or her back to health."

"I don't know whether your grandparents will let you keep him, Sammie. They have never had a dog around the mansion."

"Well, I see a lot of dogs around where you live, Amy."

"Yes, but that's around our house and farm, not around the mansion, Sammie."

"I'm going to ask my grandma anyway, and I'm sure she'll let me have it, that is if the puppy is okay. See you later, Amy and you too, Beverly."

Beverly had tears in her eyes, "Is the puppy going to die?"

"I don't think so," related Amy to her little sister.

As Sammie entered the mansion, she saw her grandfather.

"I see you have a puppy, Sammie. It looks like it's hurt."

"Yes, Grandpa, a speeding car threw it out their window just after Amy, Beverly, and I had gotten off the school bus. Will you call a vet for me, Grandpa?"

"Yes, I'll do that right now." After the call, he reported, "A vet will be here in about half an hour, Sammie. Let's find a nice soft blanket for the puppy. We'll try to make him as comfortable as we can for now."

"Grandpa, if the puppy turns out to be okay, I'd like to keep him. Could I keep him, Grandpa, please?"

"Well, your grandma is the one who you'll have to ask. She makes those kinds of decisions."

"Will you put in a good word for me, Grandpa? I really would like to have this puppy."

He laughed and responded, "I'll try, Sammie."

The veterinarian arrived, and it turned out to be a lady veterinarian. "Hello, I'm Doctor Snow. Where's our little patient?"

"Hi, I'm Sammie, and I'm the one who saved the puppy after a speeding car threw the puppy out its window. Doctor Snow, this is my grandpa, Mr. O'Grady."

She then commented, "Your grandfather and I know each other, Sammie. I come out here to the ranch once in a while. Good to see you, Samuel."

"Come this way, Doctor Snow. The puppy is in the study," Sammie directed.

Doctor Snow was gentle and compassionate with the little puppy. She then expressed her findings. "It's a good thing that he probably landed in some soft grass."

"Yes, Doctor Snow, there was lots of tall grass on both sides of the highway, and that's where he landed. Amy and I had to look for him. We finally heard him whining, and that's how we found him."

"I think he's going to be fine, but I would like to take him back to my clinic and do some x-rays. I'll call you and give you a report. Maybe you would like to have this puppy, Sammie?"

"Yes, I would like to have him. My grandpa says it's up to my grandma, and I've been told that there's never been a dog here at the mansion. When you call tomorrow, Doctor Snow, I hope by then that I will know whether I can keep him or not."

"Samuel, I think I know who threw this puppy out their car window. The reason I do is that this puppy has some very distinctive markings that I've hardly ever seen on a puppy."

"Doctor Snow, can a person who does something like this have committed a crime of sorts?" asked Sammie.

"Yes, it is a crime, Sammie. What kind of car was it that you saw?"

"It was a light blue car, but I don't know the make of the car."

"That's confirms it, Sammie. Those are the people who bring their dog into my clinic, and the last time they came, they also brought this little puppy in for his first shots."

"I hope you call the police, Doctor Snow!" commented Sammie.

"I plan to Sammie. They need to pay for this terrible thing that they did to this poor little puppy."

Later that afternoon, she saw her grandma, "Grandma, I guess you've heard all about the puppy that got thrown out of a car window, and that Amy and I saved it."

"Yes, Sammie, I did hear about it. I also know you are aware that it will now be my decision as to whether or not you get to keep him, right?"

"Yes, Grandma, I know I need your permission to have this dog. Can I please, please, keep him, please?"

"Who is going to feed the puppy? Who will take him for his walks? Where will he sleep? I'm certainly not going to do any of these things. You're busy with school and your friends, and you may not be able to care for this puppy alone."

"So you're saying that I *can't* have him, Grandma?"

"I've thought about this a lot, Sammie. I've called a meeting of all my staff. They should be coming here shortly. I said 3:00 p.m., and it's almost that time now."

"Here they come, Grandma."

There were Maria, Joseph, Justine, and Doris.

Sadie, Sammie's grandmother, spoke. "Thank you for coming. It seems that our Sammie wants a puppy, but I can't and will not take care of any puppy. If you will help take care of the puppy and organize a schedule to make sure it's fed and walked every day, then I will allow her to have the puppy."

They all smiled, and Joseph declared, "We've all talked about this. We think the new puppy can be here for all of us to enjoy."

"Well, Sammie, it looks like we'll all have a new puppy in our mansion," smiled her grandmother.

"Oh, thank you so much, everyone. I know we'll all get to love this new little addition."

"What about a name for him, Sammie?" prodded Maria.

"Let's all write down what we think we should call him, and I'll review it and choose a name."

Later that evening, Sammie had seventeen names. She finally picked Rufus, and most of the staff approved.

Sammie ran to call Amy to tell her the news.

Sammie did find out about the people who threw the dog out the window, and they were in trouble with the laws of the state. Whether she would ever hear any more about it was doubtful.

Dr. Snow called the next morning and told Sammie that the puppy was okay and that she could come to get him anytime she wanted.

Chapter Sixteen

Trouble

It was almost November, and the grapefruit would be starting its harvesting from November to April. The Fallglo Tangerines would start being harvested also in November, followed by the Dancy Tangerines in December.

In December, the Cara Cara and Clementine Oranges would also be harvested. The ranch was coming into a very busy time. Melvin Robinson, the ranch foreman, along with Samuel O'Grady and his son Simon O'Grady pretty well, ran the ranch and were hoping that they could find enough pickers for this busy time of the year.

It was nearing Christmas time, and Sammie and her friends were getting excited.

In just three more weeks, the kids would have a two-week vacation from their school work.

One afternoon, while the bus was taking the kids back to their homes, Rebecca asked Sammie, "Have you asked yet what you want for Christmas?"

"No, I've been thinking about that, and I just don't know what I want to ask for yet. My mother doesn't have much money of her own, but my grandfather gives her a little for helping around the ranch. My grandparents always give me too much, but I don't complain," she laughed. "Besides that, my grandparents in London always send gifts as well.

"Have you asked for anything for Christmas, Rebecca?"

"Yes, I want a new bike. You know the one that I ride from my house to yours every so often is so old and is falling apart."

Soon the bus stopped at the citrus ranch, and Amy, Beverly, and Sammie got off.

"See you tomorrow, Rebecca," shouted Sammie.

Before leaving, Amy asked, "Sammie, are you going to help with the harvesting this afternoon?"

"Yes, Amy. I'm going to change out of my school clothes as soon as I reach the mansion. We are going to the grapefruit and tangerine groves, right?"

"Yes, that's right, Sammie. It's quite a walk. I'll have someone come and get you, okay?"

"Thanks, Amy. I'll see you shortly, then."

As Sammie entered the mansion, Rufus, their dog, was there to meet her. She then saw Maria. "Are you hungry, Sammie?"

"Yes, Marie. I'm going to be helping with the harvesting of the grapefruit this afternoon. I'm going up to change my clothes now. I'll be back down shortly. I am getting a little hungry at that."

As she was finishing her snack, Logan walked in the backdoor of the kitchen. "Hi, Logan! I haven't seen you for a while," Sammie remarked.

"I have been really swamped, Sammie. I'm either working around the farm or helping with the citrus harvests."

"So, what brings you to the mansion house?" inquires Maria.

"I'm here to take Sammie to the grapefruit harvesting."

"Are you old enough to drive a car, Logan? If you're driving a car, I'm not going with you," cried Sammie.

"Silly girl, anyone at any age can drive a car or truck on their private land. Besides, I'm not taking you over there in a car. You'll come with me on my motorcycle. And, Sammie, *I am* old enough to drive now."

"Okay, Logan, but don't you go too fast, promise?"

"All right, Sammie. I'll be good and go slow, just for you," he responded.

Logan loved to be a tease and did go a little faster at times. They finally arrived at their destination.

"Sammie," shouted Amy, "come over this way with me. It will be dark in about an hour or so."

"Sometimes I wonder why we come out here in the fall when it gets dark so early, but I guess every little bit helps. I don't mind helping, Amy, I really don't."

That evening after she had finished her homework, Sammie was watching TV. She then heard her grandmother yelling. "Help, help, I think Samuel is having a heart attack." She had already called 911. She then said to those who came, "It's so far out here. I'm afraid of what might happen to him without immediate help.".

Finally, an ambulance arrived. By then, Samuel was resting a little more comfortably and seemed to be okay.

After examining him, the medics suggested he come back with them in the ambulance for a complete examination. They wanted a doctor to check for a slight stroke.

They took him to a nearby hospital. The following day he was released and was told he had to rest and step down from a lot of the work and decisions at the ranch to lower his stress levels.

After a couple of days, he called for his foreman, Melvin, and his son, Simon, to meet with him. "I've called this meeting because of my health problems. You both will have to do more to keep things up. I'll still be in charge for as long as I can. We'll have these meetings when I think they're needed."

"Samuel," stated Melvin, "I have some very well qualified men who have been with the ranch for a long time. I think we can use them to help free me up for other areas of the ranch."

"That is a great idea, Melvin. You go ahead with whoever you want," responded Samuel.

Sammie was close by and heard most of what they discussed. She was so happy that her grandfather was trying to take the doctor's advice and slow down.

Chapter Seventeen

Traveling to?

Summer was fast approaching, and school would soon be over. Sammie's birthday was almost here as well, and she would be turning twelve.

Sammie thought, "Next year, I'll be a teenager!"

Sammie was wondering what she would be doing this summer, hopefully not just working on the ranch most every day. She told Justine, who walked the dog each morning, that she would help her with walking Rufus when school was out for the summer as she had done before.

With Sammie's birthday approaching, her mother was always trying to make it special for her. This year Sammie decided to invite some boys too. One of the boy's names was Jason. Sammie had a crush on him, but she never told anyone about it. Her birthday was fun, and she felt more grown up with the boys added.

It was a Monday morning just two days after Sammie's birthday. Sammie was eating breakfast by herself. The phone rang and rang. She wondered where everyone was. She finally answered it.

"Hello, Sammie, this is Grandma Larson in London. I am *so* glad to have caught you. You're just the person I wanted to speak to."

"Hi, Grandma. How are you and Grandpa?"

"We're fine, Sammie. I have a surprise for you. It will be a late birthday present."

"What is it, Grandma? Please tell me!"

"We are inviting you and your mother to come to London for ten days. We will be paying for everything. Your grandfather said it would be the same cost if we had come to see you. He also said that this way, you will get to see us, and you'll get to see London too."

"That's *wonderful*, Grandma! I can hardly wait. How soon will we be coming?"

"You'll come after you finish school, Sammie. Your school's out about the end of May, right?"

"Yes, Grandma, that's right. We get out of school on the 27th of May, in just two days from now."

"We have you booked on an airline on June 14th. Your flight leaves Orlando at 10:27 a.m."

"I'm so excited to finally see you in person. Seeing you and Grandpa on Face Time has been great, but in person, it will be much better. I was wondering why your gifts hadn't arrived as they usually did."

"Well, now you know why. I must go now, Sammie. We will be in contact with you before then. Love you. Bye now."

Sammie then told Maria about the news.

Sammie started to run to find her mother, but first, Maria said, "Sammie, your mother is with Lester at the stables. Your bus will be here in less than a half-hour, so you'd better finish getting ready for school. I'll tell your mother about your news."

"Oh, Maria, I wanted to tell my mom this news, but you're right." She then ran upstairs, finishing getting herself ready.

When Sammie got to school, she was telling everyone about going to see her other grandparents in London, England.

After school, she couldn't wait to get home. She wondered if her mother would be as happy about going to see her grandparents in London as she was. Sammie was only three when they came to her daddy's funeral, so she certainly didn't remember them.

Sammie couldn't find her mother anywhere. She then ran to the kitchen. "Maria, where's my mom?"

"She's in your grandmother's bedroom."

"Is my grandma okay, Maria?"

"Yes, Sammie, she's fine. She just had a little dizzy spell. She seems to be fine now."

Sammie then ran up to her grandma's room. "Grandma, are you okay?"

"Yes, my darling, I am now."

"Mom, I guess you heard the news about us going to London."

"Yes, Sammie! I think I'm more excited than you are. I can't wait to see your other grandparents again. That's your mother's parents, you know. Can you remember your mother's name, Sammie?"

"Yes, Mom, of course, I know their names. My mother's name was Sophia, and my father's name was Cody."

"Yes, Sammie, that's right. Now, we still have about two weeks before we leave. I know you've been waiting to see them in person for a very long time, and now you will," her mother smiled.

Sammie's mother was spending a lot of time with Lester at the stables. Sammie began wondering if Lester would be her new father. Her mother sure seemed to like him.

"Mom, could you come to my bedroom? I want to talk to you."

"Yes, that will be fine, Sammie."

"Glad your feeling better, Grandma. I'll see you later."

After leaving her grandma, she entered her room with her mother. They both sat on Sammie's bed. "Mother, I can't believe that my grandparents haven't tried to visit me before now. The first time they saw me was when I was three, and that was *nine* years ago. I know that they have sent cards and gifts and phoned me."

"And you don't think that was enough, do you, Sammie?"

"No, I don't, Mother! I almost feel like refusing to accept their invitation, but I, of course, won't. It still makes me mad that they couldn't find the time to come. No one can be that busy!"

"You shouldn't be judging them, Sammie. They may have had a good reason for not coming these last nine years. It is very expensive to fly to Florida from London."

"Maybe so, Mother. I also wanted to ask you about your relationship with Lester. Is there something going on with you two?"

"Well, Sammie, Lester, and I have grown very fond of each other."

"Does that mean you may want to marry him?"

"Maybe, we've talked about it," her mother responded.

"If you marry him, Mother, you and I would have to move out of the mansion house and go and live with him, wouldn't we?"

"Yes, that would be true, Sammie."

Her mother continued, " Now, Sammie, with regards to our trip to London. I have to confess that I'm still a little afraid to travel, especially overseas. I don't like big cities and big airports. I wouldn't know what to do or where to go."

"Mom, Joseph will take us to the airport."

"I wouldn't know where to go after he'd dropped us off. I know, I'll ask Sadie, your grandmother, if she can give me any ideas on how to help me with this problem of mine."

It was about an hour later, and she saw Sadie sitting in their library reading. Good to see you up and around, Sadie. I have a problem. I don't know even how to explain it."

"Sit down here next to me. Now, tell me about your problem, Kate."

"Sadie, I'm afraid to go to a large airport in the big city like Orlando. I wouldn't know where to go or even where to find my flight."

"Kate, everything will be fine at the airport. There are a lot of people there who will help you. I know you will love London when you get there. Samuel and I have been there twice, and we enjoyed it. When you came here to Orlando from your home town, everything went okay, right?"

"Yes, but Simon was right there to greet Sammie and me and got our luggage for us. He then took us to the ranch. We didn't have to worry about anything. I also didn't like riding on a plane. Sadie, I'm used to living in a small town. Davis and I hated big cities. I'm afraid to go to airports."

Sadie smiled, "Kate, let me call Hannah, Simon's wife. I think she will go with you to the airport and be your guide. All you will have to do is to follow Hannah. She'll take care of everything."

Sadie then called Hannah. "Hannah, this is Sadie. Sammie and Kate have just been invited to visit London. Now Sammie can finally meet her other grandparents. Kate is deathly afraid of big cities and airports. She would like a guide. Are you free on June 14th... Yes, Hannah, I'll wait while you check your calendar...Great, Hannah, I know Kate will sure enjoy you helping her. I'll take care of Kassie while you're gone."

"Sadie, I am so glad when we first came here that you encouraged us to get passports. I sure never thought we would ever use them. Thank you, now that's *one* thing we won't have to worry about."

"Kate, I'm glad that you're going to have this new experience. Maybe this will help you get used to big airports and big cities."

"Sadie, after Sammie and I decided to come here to the ranch, I was happy because your ranch is far away from cities," Kate laughed.

When Sammie heard that Hannah was going to be their guide, she was so happy that her mother wouldn't be so worried about everything.

Sammie began thinking about her future. What if her mother was to marry Lester? Having a birthday party at Lester's house and not at the mansion house would be strange. Would any of her friends even come? She didn't even know where Lester lived. Maybe she could stay in the mansion house with her grandparents.

June 14th had finally arrived. Sammie and her mother had been packing for at least two days before their trip to London. Their flight was to leave at 10:30 a.m., so they had to leave early to be there four hours ahead of their flight time.

Kate thanked Hannah for being there for them. She couldn't go through security or passport control, but she explained what would happen.

"Have a wonderful time. I'll be here waiting for you when you return," cried Hannah.

As they were called to board the plane, her mother commented, "Well, are you still a little disturbed with your grandparents, Sammie?"

"I guess I really shouldn't be, should I, Mother?"

It was a long flight that would take about nine hours, but they kept busy playing video games, watching a movie, and doing some reading. It was fun to have meals served on the plane. That didn't happen when they flew to Florida.

Their flight was finally landing in London. Sammie now was getting excited to see her grandparents.

As they came into the waiting area, they saw them. Sammie's Grandmother welcomed her with open arms.

After William and Rachel had given Kate and Sammie a lot of hugs, they went and got their luggage and then proceeded to the parking garage. They then all departed the terminal and were soon on their way back to their home. It seemed odd to be driving on the opposite side of the road, and the steering wheel being on the right of the car.

Sammie didn't know what they would see while they were there and wished she and her mother had planned better about things that they may be seeing. Sammie also hoped her grandparents would take them to their university, where they both worked. She didn't know very much about *the University of London.*

On the way to their home, her Grandfather Larson remarked, "Tomorrow, we'll show you what we have planned for you to see while you're here."

Her grandparents didn't appear to be very well off. Their car was just an ordinary car. When they got to their home, it was very nice, but nothing like what they were used to, like the mansion where they lived. They did have two lovely guest rooms that were perfect for her and her mother.

Chapter Eighteen

London and?

That afternoon and evening were wonderful. Sammie was happy finally having the chance to get to know her other grandparents.

"Grandpa, can you take us to see *The University of London* where you and grandma work?"

"Yes, we will include that in what you'll be seeing, Sammie. Well, it's getting late," her grandfather remarked. "I'm sure you're both tired after that long flight from Florida. Sleep as long as you want to. We can have breakfast anytime you are ready for it. With the time change, it takes a while for your body to adjust."

In the morning, as Sammie was waking, she smelled something wonderful. She looked at her watch. "Oh, it's past 9:00 a.m.! Was her grandma making breakfast?" she wondered. She must be as Sammie hadn't seen any servants around. She was sure that they didn't have any. She jumped up and ran into her mother's room, but she wasn't in her room.

Just then, she heard her mother, "Sammie, I see you. Get your robe on and come down to breakfast. Your grandmother and I have prepared a wonderful breakfast for you. Your grandfather is already down here."

She went and got her robe on and ran down the stairs and into the kitchen. "Good morning, everyone."

"Good morning, Sammie," her grandmother stated. "Sit down right over there next to your grandpa. Your mother and I have made lots of things this morning. There are eggs, English bacon, pancakes, oatmeal, regular dry cereal, and sweet rolls."

"Wow, I feel like I'm in a restaurant. I am hungry. I'll have scrambled eggs, bacon, toast, and pancakes. What is English bacon?"

"English bacon is more like ham. You'll like it." Replied her grandmother.

As Sammie's Grandfather was eating, he informed them of the things they would be doing.

"This afternoon, we are going to take you on a sightseeing boat tour. It's called the Thames River Cruise. There are many of these cruises available. We can show you a lot of London, or at least some of the highlights around our town, from this boat."

"That sounds great, right, Sammie?" her mother responded.

Her grandpa continued, "There is somewhere that we are going to take you to, and you'll never guess where. It's something you may not have ever thought possible while you were visiting us here in London."

"I couldn't even guess what it might be, Grandpa! Please tell us!" begged Sammie.

"How would you like to go to Paris, France?"

"Oh, Mr. Larson, we could never ask you to take us to Paris. Just seeing you both is enough, along with some sightseeing here in London," cried Kate.

Sammie's grandma added, "You've probably never heard of the Eurostar train. It's a train that goes part of the way under the ocean and goes from London to Paris. It goes 186 miles per hour and can get to Paris in only two and a quarter hours. We are going to take you both to *Paris* tomorrow."

"That almost seems impossible! Even to think that a train can go that fast, Grandma!" responded Sammie.

That afternoon, they saw so much from the boat cruise. They even got to ride on the famous double-decker buses. That evening they had a nice dinner at one of the restaurants near their home. Kate saw the prices on the menu in pounds, not in dollars. It was hard to tell how much things really did cost in dollars.

Late that evening as Sammie was getting ready for bed, her mother came into her room. "Sammie, can you believe we'll be in Paris, France tomorrow?"

"No, mom, it really is hard to believe. I'll sure have a lot to tell my friends."

In the morning after breakfast, Sammie's grandfather called a cab to take them to the Eurostar train station. When they got there, the station was huge. There were trains all over the place going to many various locations outside of London.

They finally were aboard the Eurostar train and on their way to Paris. Her grandpa began telling her more about the train. "Sammie, its' 307 miles to Paris, and as your grandma had told you before, it goes a 186 miles per hour. That's how we can get there so fast. We'll be going into a tunnel shortly that will take us under the ocean. We'll be in the tunnel for about twenty minutes."

Her grandma then added, "Sammie, there's a Disneyland by Paris, but because you live about an hour from Disney World in Florida, we didn't think you'd want to see it in Paris."

"No, Grandma, you're right. I'm sure it's about the same as the one in Florida."

As they went through the tunnel, it was a little scary, and twenty minutes seemed a lot longer to Sammie. Finally, they arrived in Paris!

"Sammie, we can't see everything. That would take days, but we thought we'd go to the Eiffel Tower today. The Tower was built in 1889. If you wanted to take the stairs, there are 1665 steps to the top, but I think we'll take the elevator," her grandfather laughed.

He continued, "Then we'll go to see the famous Triumphal Arch. Napoleon commissioned it. Lastly, we can take the cruise on the Seine River at night. I have also made reservations at a nice hotel. Tomorrow, we'll go see the Louvre Museum and then head back home on the Eurostar train."

Kate then pulled William aside, "Your spending way too much on us. I never expected you to do all of this. We still have a lot to see in London."

He smiled and responded, "Kate, we've been saving for nine years."

Everything they saw was terrific. It seemed impossible that they were in Paris seeing all these beautiful things. Their day was perfect.

That night Kate was so tired. She asked William if they could sleep a little longer.

"Yes, Kate, I'm exhausted too, and so is Rachel. Let's try to be ready by at least 9:30 a.m., and we'll eat breakfast down in the hotel's restaurant."

The Louvre Museum was unbelievable. It was so educational for Sammie. They spent the rest of the morning there, had lunch, and returned for another three hours in the museum. Finally, it was time to take the Eurostar train back to London. Sammie slept almost all the way back.

The next morning they all slept in, being so very tired from their wonderful Paris trip.

In the morning, Sammie's grandmother declared, "Today we're all staying home to recoup from our Paris trip. Sammie, I'm going to show you some of our family pictures. We have a lot of pictures of your mother as she was growing up with us. We were so happy when we heard that your daddy's brother had decided to raise you and love you. Sometimes we regret that we didn't step up and take you."

Sammie was so happy to see all the pictures of her mother. She only had one photo of her mother and father, and that was the day they got married.

They all spent the rest of the morning looking through the pictures. Sammie's grandmother told her a lot about her mother from the time she was born until she left home for college.

Sammie had never been so happy to see all those pictures of her mother. "Sammie," her grandma commented, "If you would like, you may pick out some photos of your mother from my scrapbooks. I have so many, so please pick out the ones you would like to take back with you to Florida."

"Well, this is the fifth day of the ten days you have here. I have a lot more planned for you," said William, Sammie's grandfather.

"What will we see today?" Sammie asked him.

"We are going to take you to Warner Brothers Studio. They have a tour to see all kinds of things, including the making of the Harry Potter movies. Since it's late morning already, we'll go and have an early lunch and then do the tour at the studio."

"Are we going to do anything this evening?" inquired Sammie.

"Yes, we are going to take you to ride on the London's Eye, a giant Ferris wheel. It is the tallest cantilevered observation wheel in Europe. Each big cabin holds about twenty people and is air-conditioned. There are a lot of these cabins on this Ferris wheel. You can see a lot of London at night. It's awesome. The Ferris wheel goes around slowly and takes thirty minutes. You'll love it, Sammie."

In the next four days, they visited 'Madame Tussaud's Wax Museum,' cruised the river from Westminster to the Tower of London, watched the changing of the guards at Buckingham Palace, and toured the 'Natural History Museum.' They also enjoyed riding the double-decker buses again and seeing the beautiful buildings, parks, and monuments.

The ninth day came, and they were all pretty well worn out. The next morning Kate and Sammie would be flying back to Orlando.

Sammies's grandparents drove them to the airport. They said good-bye to William and hugged him. Rachel then took them into the terminal and checked them in with the airlines. She showed them were to go through security and passport control before finding the gate for their plane.

After hugs and kisses, they said there final farewell to Rachel, Sammie's Grandma, and thanked her for a wonderful ten days. When they boarded their plane, this time, Kate wasn't so scared of flying. They could rest some during the next nine hours.

Finally, they landed in Orlando. After going through passport control and customs with their luggage, they were happy to see Hannah waiting for them. She helped get their luggage to the pick-up area in front of the airport. Joseph was waiting out front for them. Soon they were home and so happy to tell everyone about all the things that they had seen and done.

Chapter Nineteen

Sammie Has to Have What?

Sammie was happy to be home and glad that she had finally gotten to know her grandparents in London so much better. She hoped it wouldn't be so long before she saw them again.

Summer was racing by, and July was so hot. Harvest time was going on for the Valencia oranges. Sammie wasn't volunteering when it was so exceptionally hot out.

Sammie and Rebecca sure used the swimming pool a lot. They invited Jennifer and Rachel over a few times. The girls were getting a little bored with summer and could hardly wait for school to start within just a couple of weeks. It would be Sammie's second year in middle school.

It was now only a week until school would be starting. It was a Thursday morning, and Sammie was waking up. She heard a soft knock on her door. "Sammie, it's time to get up. I hope you remembered that your grandma and I are going to take you shopping for your fall school clothes."

"When do I have to be ready to leave, Mother?"

"In an hour, Sammie, your breakfast is almost ready now, so hurry down, dear."

She hurriedly put on her robe and ran down to the kitchen, saying, "Good morning, everyone."

"Sammie, your friend, Rebecca, called a little bit ago and wanted to know what you both could do today. I told her we would be going shopping for your school clothes most of the day."

"Mom, can she go with us?"

"Yes, Sammie, Rebecca has already asked her mother if she could go, and her mother told her she could come with us."

"Great, Mother, with Rebecca along, it will be an extra fun day. We can help each other pick out our school clothes together."

"Yes, it will be a fun day, Sammie. I am a little concerned, though."

"Why, Mother?"

"Rebecca's parents aren't as well off as we are, Sammie. You'll be picking out a lot more clothes than she will. That may make her uncomfortable and sad."

"I know how we can solve this problem," Sammie's Grandma added. "We'll all try to keep track of both of your selections. That way, Rebecca will feel comfortable with everything you're both buying."

"That's a great idea, Grandma. I sure don't want to hurt my best friend's feelings."

"Sammie, I know you may need a lot more things for school, so you and I will go shopping in a few days again to finish getting everything that you'll need, okay?"

"Yes, Grandma, it will be wonderful to spend a day with you."

The first day of school had arrived, and Bob, their bus driver, was out in front blowing his horn. Beverly was already in front, waiting for the bus. She was only three years younger than Sammie and was now nine years old and in the fifth grade. Amy was in high school and was getting a ride from one of her friends at her school. They had to drive all the way to Melbourne.

As Sammie and Beverly entered the bus, Bob was saying, "Good morning, girls." He was always so cheerful, and everyone sure loved him.

As Sammie made her way down the aisle, she saw her friend, Rebecca, who declared, "I'm sure glad we both got to be together in most of our classes this year."

"Yes, Rebecca, I'm so happy about that too. How did we get so lucky?"

Their first class was history, and Mr. Harris was their teacher. As the class ended, Mr. Harris asked Sammie to stay after class.

"Sammie, I noticed that you were having trouble seeing the whiteboard. You were squinting, weren't you?"

"Yes, Mr. Harris, I was."

"Sammie, I want you to have your mother take you to see an optometrist. I'm sure you're going to need glasses."

When Sammie had finished all of her classes for the day, she left and headed for the bus. She was distraught. She entered the bus and sat next to her friend, Rebecca.

"What's wrong, Sammie?"

"Mr. Harris, our history teacher, said I probably would need glasses."

"Well, what's so bad about wearing glasses, Sammie?"

"It will make me feel like a goon!"

"It would not, Sammie. There are a lot of kids who wear glasses, even some at a very young age," explained Rebecca.

"Well, I'm not going to wear glasses, and that's final!"

"Aren't you even going to tell your mother what Mr. Harris asked you to do?" asked Rebecca.

"I guess I'll have to tell her, but I'll also tell her I'm not going to wear glasses!" cried Sammie.

After dinner that night, Sammie asked her mother to come into the living room.

"Is there something wrong, Sammie?"

"My history teacher, Mr. Harris, said I was squinting and that I must be having trouble seeing the board."

"Are you having trouble seeing the board, Sammie?"

"Yes, Mother, but I refuse to wear glasses! I'll look ridiculous!"

"I'll make an appointment, and we'll see what the doctor recommends we do."

"Do we have to, Mother?"

"Yes, my darling girl, we do."

Her mother did make an appointment for Sammie. She would be seeing Doctor Wells in just two days.

When they went to the doctor, he examined Sammie and declared, "Young lady, you will need glasses."

"Doctor Wells, I'm not going to wear glasses!" she almost screamed.

Her mother then asked, "Could she wear contact lenses, doctor?"

"I'm afraid not, Mrs. O'Grady. Her eyes are a little misshaped, and contacts wouldn't work for her."

Sammie left the doctor's office and went to the waiting room. She had tears running down her face. She then noticed a girl that was in her class entering with her mother.

"Hi, Stephanie. Are you here to see about glasses?" inquired Sammie.

"No, Sammie. I'm here to pick up my new glasses. Are you getting glasses, Sammie?"

"The doctor said I need glasses, but I don't want to wear glasses."

"Tomorrow, I'll have my new glasses on when I get to school," Stephanie said, smiling. "I'll want to see what you think of them. There are two other girls in our class that wear glasses, and I think they look okay."

On the way back to the mansion, her mother informed her. "The doctor said that you might only need your glasses for things far away and not so much to read. That means you're far-sighted."

"So I'll have to wear my glasses, except for reading. Mother, that means I'll be wearing them almost all the time! I'm not that bad yet, so I'm not going to get glasses, and that's that!"

The next day in class, Sammie asked, "Jane, do you mind wearing your glasses?"

She told Sammie she thought she looked better wearing them.

She then asked, "Trinity, do you like wearing glasses?"

Trinity then commented, "My mother and father made me get glasses. I hated them at first, but now I don't mind wearing them. If you get glasses, you might feel like I did at first as well."

Sammie kept thinking, "I can't see the board at school, and my grades are getting a little worse. I guess I'll *have* to wear glasses."

It was just about three weeks later that she was wearing her glasses. On her first day at school with her new glasses, a boy in her school, Marvin, remarked, "Sammie, you look weird wearing those glasses."

Sammie marched up to Marvin and punched him in the face right in front of the class. "Now, does anyone else think I look weird?"

After that, no one made any comments.

After dinner that same day, her grandfather excused himself and went to his library, which he did often. Everyone noticed that his health was failing more and more. Sammie followed him into the library.

"Grandpa, what do you think of my glasses?"

"It makes you look smarter."

"It does not, Grandpa! I am already one of the top students in my class," she laughed.

"You look just fine. Come here, and give me a hug."

"Grandpa, I am planning to stay on the ranch after I finish college. I promise!"

"I hope you will, Sammie. So many things can change when you are growing up, though."

"I won't change my mind about staying. I love this ranch, and I love you, Grandpa."

Chapter Twenty

The Letter

It was almost the end of another year at school. Sammie would be turning thirteen in May, and she could hardly wait to be a teenager.

One afternoon in late April, after Sammie and Beverly had departed the school bus, she headed for the mansion as she always did. She thought she'd check to see if the mail had come. There was a lot. Most of it was for her grandparents. She did notice a letter addressed to her mother. The return address was from Charlotte, North Carolina. The person who sent it was Melissa Stewart.

As Sammie entered the mansion, she saw her grandmother. "Grandma, my mother got a letter from a Melissa Stewart. Do you know who she is?"

"No, Sammie, I've never heard of her before. It's probably just one of your mother's friends."

"Where is my mother, Grandma?"

"She's in the kitchen, helping Maria."

Sammie then ran to the kitchen. "Mother, here's a letter that just came for you. It's from someone named Melissa Stewart."

Her mother took the letter and put it in her pocket. Thank you, Sammie."

"Who is Melissa Stewart, and how do you know her?" she asked her mother.

"It's someone who I haven't heard from for a very long time, Sammie," her mother responded.

"Aren't you going to read it, Mom?"

"I will later, Sammie."

It was Saturday afternoon, and Sammie was looking for her mom. She went into her room, but her mom wasn't there. Sammie then noticed the letter that her mother had received from this Melissa Stewart was on her bed. She was curious and wanted to know who this Melissa Stewart was. She picked up the letter and was about to open it when her mother came in.

"Sammie, would you please hand me the letter?"

"Mom, I was just curious and didn't think I was doing anything wrong. We never keep secrets from each other, right?"

"Well, what's in this letter is one secret that I never told you about, and I should have, Sammie."

"Well, can you tell me now?"

"Yes, my darling girl. Let's sit over there on that couch."

"Maybe you should just read the letter first, Mother."

"Sammie, I need to tell you things about my earlier life first. I was born into a very wealthy family in Charlotte, North Carolina. My father, Henry Stewart, was very much like your grandfather used to be."

"What was your father's business that made him so rich?"

"He owned large cotton mills, and I didn't see him very often."

"What about your mother?"

"My mother's name was Melissa Stewart."

Sammie then shouted, "That's the lady who sent you the letter. She's your mother?"

"Yes, Sammie."

It finally dawned on Sammie, and she shouted, "I have other grandparents?

"Yes, Sammie. I'm so sorry I never told you about them before now. My mother wasn't at all a very loving mother to me. When I was growing up, my mother hired a tutor for me. I never had any children to play in that big mansion of ours. When I was eight, my parents shipped me off to a private school for girls and then later to a high school again with girls only."

"I'm sure glad that you and my grandparents never did that to me. I love being around family."

"When I was a senior in that private high school, I ran away and hid at one of my friend's home."

"Did they ever find you?"

"Yes, Sammie, my father found me about two months later. I told my father that I would keep running away if they put me back in that all-girls school."

"Did he agree? I bet he didn't," cried Sammie.

"He did agree, which surprised me. In my senior year, I went to a regular public high school. That's where I met Davis. He was a policeman that was around our school a lot. After I graduated, Davis and I started dating. My father tried to put a stop to it. He wanted me to work in his company, and to marry a wealthy man. He didn't like me dating a common policeman."

"Well, I know you married Davis, so what did your father do when you disobeyed him?"

"He said he would disinherit me if I married Davis, and that he would no longer allow me ever to call him Father. My mother agreed with him, and I have never seen them since."

"So, Mom, how did they know where you were?"

"I always let them know about important things, like Davis being shot and killed in his work as a police officer. They, of course, didn't come to the funeral. I also kept them informed about where I was living."

"Mom, can we read the letter now?"

"No, Sammie, there is a lot that is personal, but it says that my father is dying from cancer and only has a few weeks to live."

"Do they want you to come to be with him after all these years?"

"Yes, Sammie, they do. My mother says she is also in very poor health too."

"Are you going to go?"

"I don't know, probably, Sammie."

"Mother, why didn't you ever tell me about your parents? I guess I just never thought about having other grandparents. I should have figured that out for myself. If you go, can I go with you, Mom?"

"At this point, Sammie, I don't even know if I want to go. If I don't go, I'll be acting just like they always did. I guess I don't want to be like that, either."

Kate sent a telegram to her mother saying that she was coming in three days, and was bringing her daughter, Sammie, with her.

They flew to Charlotte, North Carolina, and then took a taxi to the Stewart Estate.

As they arrived, Sammie commented, "Wow, Mother, look how beautiful and how big the estate is. I think it's much bigger than the O'Grady Estate."

"Yes, Sammie, it's huge all right," responded her mother.

Soon they were at the front door ringing the bell. A butler answered the door.

"Miss Kate, welcome. It's good to see you after all these years."

Just then, Kate saw her mother coming down the big staircase. She stopped about halfway down, saying, "Kate, come upstairs."

Kate followed her mother up the stairs with Sammie trailing behind. When Kate got to her father's bedside, he said, "My Kate, I'm so glad you came. I wouldn't have blamed you if you hadn't come."

Kate then responded, "You're still my father. I was so upset and hurt when you disowned me. I still loved you both, even though you made it hard for me to do so."

Her mother then stated, "Kate, my daughter, I want to thank you so much for coming. I told your father, 'Kate won't come.'"

Mother, Father, this is Sammie. She wanted to come to be with me. In one of my letters so long ago, I told you that we adopted her when she was just three. She was Cody and Sophie's little girl. They both had drowned in a lake during a terrible storm."

Kate's father then spoke, "Kate, I have willed everything to you. You can step in and help manage things, or you can sell everything. Anything you decide to do is fine with me. Your mother agrees with my decision on this. She has more than enough money to live on until she passes, and then you'll have everything that's left of hers as well."

"Father, why have you both waited until it's almost too late for us to enjoy each other?" cried Kate.

"I guess some of us think the end will never come, and if it does, oh well," her father added.

"Why are you leaving all of your wealth to me, Father?"

"Who else is there, Kate?"

Before she left, Kate informed her mother, "I will be back for the funeral." She then kissed her, and they left the vast Stewart estate where she had grown up as a little girl so long ago.

As Sammie and her mother were flying back to Orlando, Sammie remarked, "Mother, you were raised in a wealthy estate, and will receive a great deal of money. My grandfather O'Grady has put you and me in his will too, and I will be rich just like you."

"Sammie, I just don't know what I'm going to do with all this unexpected money."

When they finally got back to the O'Grady's estate, they were warmly received. Kate then asked to see both Samuel and Sadie privately.

Samuel asked Kate to come into his office. Sadie was there as well. "How is your father, Kate?"

"He only has days left. Samuel, he has willed me everything. He said I could help oversee things in his businesses or just sell everything. He also said when his wife, my mother, passes, I will inherit all of her wealth as well. My father further related that I would be receiving between one billion three hundred million, or one billion five hundred million."

"That, Kate is a lot of money, even way more than I have," Samuel informed her.

"I just don't know what to do with that huge amount of money. Could you help me or point me to someone who can give me some sound advice?"

It was just eleven days later that her father passed away. They felt like they had just returned to Florida from North Carolina, now it was time to return again for his funeral.

After the funeral, Kate informed her mother that she would like her to sell everything and come and live on the O'Grady Estate with them. Her mother said she would think about it.

When she returned to the O'Grady estate, she went to the stables to see Lester. He, of course, had heard all that was going on with Kate. He was a little disturbed that she hadn't come to him for his advice.

As she entered, she saw him brushing one of the horses. "Well, Kate, I'm glad you finally found time to come up to the stables to see me."

"I see that you're upset with me, Lester. I have had my whole life being turned upside down. I haven't been able to think straight or even sleep at night."

"I would have thought you would have turned to me first, being as we were so close to one another!"

"Well, Lester, I am here now, and you're my priority. I'm I forgiven?"

"Yes, my darling Kate. Come here."

It was about three weeks later when she found out that she had inherited 1.4 billion dollars. She knew she would also be receiving even more when her mother passed away.

Sammie was glad that she had gone to see Henry and Melissa Stewart, her other grandparents. Kate again invited her mother to come and spend the rest of her life in Florida close to them, but her mother had decided she didn't want to leave everything she had grown accustomed to for so long.

Chapter Twenty-One

Money, Money, and Lester

It was now May, and Sammie wanted a big party for her upcoming thirteenth birthday. She asked her mother if she could have her birthday party someplace other than the mansion.

"Sammie, you've always had your birthday parties here, at the mansion house. Why would you want to go someplace else?"

"Mom, you have over a billion dollars. What about Disney World? They have places for parties."

"Sammie, I don't want to be showing off our new wealth. People don't like show-offs, and that's just what they will think if you plan a party at Disney World."

"Then plan something super special for my thirteenth birthday. Make it a surprise."

"Okay, Sammie, I'll try and think of something that isn't too showy."

When Sammie went to school the next day and said something about her thirteenth birthday party, almost everyone didn't even sound excited about coming.

One boy in her class said, "Well, Miss rich girl, now you're doubly rich with your grandfather and now your mother's money, will you still be coming to our school?"

Sammie then replied, "Yes, Tommy, I still intend to come to this school. My mother plans on helping a lot of people with her money."

That night after dinner, Sammie asked her grandfather, "Grandfather, the kids at school are treating me differently now that my mother has a lot of money. Even some of my best friends are acting a little strange."

"Some of your friends are thinking you're better than they are now, Sammie. They think you should be with other rich people, not them."

"But, Grandfather, I don't think that way! I was hoping to have a party, something maybe special for my thirteenth birthday. Now I'm wondering if anyone will even want to come to my party!"

"Maybe you should have your party at Rebecca's house and invite just your close friends. That way, they won't think you're a big show-off after-all."

"That's a great idea, Grandpa! I'll ask Rebecca if I can have a party at her house."

Sammie called her friend. "Rebecca, this is Sammie. My thirteenth birth is coming up, as you know. Could we have it at your house?"

"Why would you want to have it at my house, Sammie? You invite tons of kids. My house isn't big enough for the kind of parties you always have."

"Rebecca, the kids at school are treating me, well, not like they used to. Even you're a little that way."

"I'm sorry, Sammie, I didn't mean to, but being so rich makes you act a little different too, and I don't like it, and neither do the kids."

"I didn't think I was acting differently, Rebecca."

"Well, you are, Sammie. All you do is talk about you going to Charlotte, North Carolina, and your other grandfather giving your mother tons of money. Also, about how rich you're going to be when you are part owner of the O'Grady Citrus Ranch."

"I guess I have been talking too much about me and making my classmates feel like they're nobodies."

"Sammie, if I have a party for you at my house, you won't be able to invite very many of your friends."

"I know, Rebecca, but please ask your mother. My mom will help too."

Sammie did have her party at Rebecca's, and it was great. The kids at school started to return to normal, which now made Sammie so happy.

It was a Saturday morning, and Sammie, Rebecca, and Rachel were planning a trip to Orlando to do some shopping for their summer clothes. Rebecca's mother was taking them. The girls had a marvelous time shopping for their summer clothes. It was such fun.

Then Rachel laughed, saying, "Now, we can be sure that none of us will look alike."

Lester and Kate, Sammie's mother, were becoming closer in the last few weeks. Lester had wanted to ask Kate to go out for dinner, so he finally called and invited her to go to dinner with him that Saturday. The closest town was Rockledge, which is where Lester lived. They had a nice restaurant there. It was the same Saturday that Sammie and her friends went shopping in Orlando.

Lester picked Kate up at the mansion house in his old pickup truck. She was dressed up, but not too much. Lester was dressed about the same at Kate.

When they got to the restaurant and had ordered Lester addressed her. "Kate, with your now having all this money, I hope it doesn't change things between us."

"No, Lester, not at all. Never think that."

"Kate a few weeks ago, Samuel, called me into his office to talk with me. This was before you got all this money."

"What did he want to talk to you about?"

"He asked me if I intended to marry you."

"What did you say, Lester?"

"Kate, let me finish. He then told me that if I married you, I would be included in the O'Grady family. He said I would help Simon and Melvin run the ranch because he really couldn't help any more the way he used to."

Lester paused and then said, "Kate, will you marry me?"

"Yes! Yes! Yes! I will, Lester."

There were lots of hugs and kisses. "Kate, now, let's talk about all the money that you've received."

"Lester, when we get married, all that money will be yours too. You can help me in knowing what to do with *our* money."

When they got back to the mansion house, they found Samuel and Sadie watching TV. They then told them about their engagement.

Sadie yelled, "Congratulations! Have you set a date yet?"

"No, Sadie, but we will in a few days," responded Kate.

Samuel exclaimed, "We will make this the biggest wedding ever."

When Sammie finally got back from their shopping in Orlando, she had Rebecca and her mother with her. "Mother, can Rebecca and I have a sleepover, please? Rebecca's mother says it's okay with her."

"Yes, you may." Kate then turned to Sarah, Rebecca's mother. "It's good to see you, Sarah. Thanks so much for taking the girls shopping. I hope they didn't wear you out too much."

"No, not at all, Kate. I loved being with the girls," she replied. She then left.

Kate then spoke, "Sammie, we have an announcement to make. Lester has asked me to marry him, and I, of course, said *yes*."

Sammie then rushed over to her mother, "I'm happy for you, Mother." She also hugged Lester.

Sammie and Rebecca then ran up to her room. "I knew this was coming, and I'm not sure of my feelings, Rebecca. Is that wrong?"

"I don't think so, Sammie. It will be a big change for you. I've seen Lester's little house down in Rockledge. I guess that's where you'll be living for a while, right?"

"I'm not sure, but with all the money they have, they could buy anything. I bet Lester will build a bigger mansion than my grandpa's."

Lester and Kate were married, and afterward, the O'Grady's put on a very lovely reception for them.

Now, as to where Lester and Kate would live. Samuel, Sammie's grandfather, invited them to live in the mansion until they could build their own home. They quickly agreed to his invitation. The O'Grady Citrus Ranch had lots of other lands around the ranch, and that's where Lester and Kate would be making their new home. Samuel wanted Kate and Sammie O'Grady to live on his property. Oh, and now Kate has a new name, Kate Klein.

Sammie was so glad that she was going to get to stay in the mansion house and would be able to keep her same bedroom. She knew it would take some time to accept Lester as her step-father though.

Chapter Twenty-Two

Sandra Cunningham

School was now over, and Sammie was glad that her mother was happy, now that she was married. Her mother, Kate, was thinking now she would have time to explore her drawing and do some painting again. She wanted to have a room in their new mansion where she could do these things again.

Lester always treated Kate and Sammie well. Sammie was getting used to Lester a little more.

One afternoon, Sammie's cell phone rang. "Hi, Sammie. I'm bored. Let's do something," whined Rebecca.

"Why don't you ride your new bike over here, and we'll try to figure out something to do, okay?" replied Sammie.

"All right, I'll see you soon."

After Rebecca got there, Sammie commented, "Rebecca, I've been thinking about Sandra Cunningham."

"What made you think of her, Sammie?"

"I always feel so sorry for her. The clothes she wears are awful, and she has no friends, Rebecca."

"Sammie, there are lots of poor people, but you can't help them all."

"Rebecca, she's one of our classmates. There must be *something* we can do, but what?"

"Well, Sammie, you're rich, and now, your mother is very wealthy too. Just take her shopping and let her buy anything she wants."

"Oh, that would be great. What about Millie, her little sister, who is in the first grade. We can't leave her out. I can see it all now, Rebecca. Their two little girls are now dressed in their new beautiful clothes, and her parents are not even dressed as well as their girls."

"Sammie, I don't have an answer for you," cried Rebecca."

"I'm determined to find some way to help Sandra's whole family. I'm going to ask my mom and my grandpa about this problem. Maybe they can help in some way."

"I know, and it can't be giving them money, right, Sammie?"

"That's right, Rebecca, and that's why it's such a puzzle."

The girls swam and played games and had a wonderful time together that afternoon.

That same night she went to her grandpa's office. "Grandpa, I have a problem, and I can't seem to get an answer. I hoped maybe you could give me some ideas on maybe how to solve this."

"Well, this sounds serious. Tell me your problem, Sammie."

"I have a friend in my class at school. Her name is Sandra Cunningham. Do you know this family?"

"No, I don't, Sammie. Why is this girl posing a problem for you?"

"Sandra's family is impoverished. Sandra and her little sister, Millie, are always dressed so poorly. They also have no friends and are teased and laughed at while they're at school. I was wondering how I could somehow help their family, Grandpa."

"Sammie, giving them money won't help. There are so many poor people. We couldn't just help one."

"I know, Grandpa. Money wouldn't help, it would only embarrass them to be taking charity. That's my problem, Grandpa."

"I don't have an answer for you, Sammie. I wish I did."

"Thanks, Grandpa. I still think there must be an answer, and I'm going to keep trying to find it."

Sammie then went to say good-night to her mother and step-father. She then explained the problem to them both.

"Sammie, what's the family's name?" asked Lester.

"It's Cunningham, Lester."

"I know that name, but I can't remember too much about them. Wait, I just remembered. Ryan Cunningham was working in the post office. I heard that he quit. I know that Ryan worked for years with horses and knows everything about how to care for them."

"Lester, maybe Mr. Cunningham can come and work here at the stables. He can take your place."

"That's right, Sammie. I'm still trying to help run the ranch and the stables. Ryan would be just the right person, Sammie."

Sammie was so pleased that she hadn't given up on trying to help the Cunningham's.

Lester went to the Cunningham's home after getting permission from Mr. O' Grady to hire him. He found that Mr. Cunningham was at home.

"Ryan, I'm Lester Kline. I work for the O'Grady's. I just married Kate O'Grady. My job on the ranch was taking care of the stables, and looking after a small herd of cows. Now that I'm married to an O'Grady, Mr. O'Grady has promoted me to help run the ranch."

"I'm happy for you, Lester, but why are you here today?"

"I'm here to hire you as our new stableman. It pays very well. You will be provided with a nice home to live in at no charge to you."

Ryan began to get a big smile on his face. "Yes, I accept your offer, Lester. Am I dreaming? I can't believe what's happening."

"Great, you can start tomorrow if you would like. Be at the ranch stables at 9:00 a.m."

"I'll be there, Lester."

The next morning Ryan was there. He had brought his daughters, Millie and Sandra, with him.

"I hope it's okay that I brought my daughters with me. They begged me so hard that I couldn't say no. Our whole family is so happy about my new job on 'The O'Grady's Citrus Ranch.'"

Lester welcomed his two daughters, giving them big hugs. He then called Sammie on his cell phone, asking her to come to the stables.

When Sammie got to the stables, she saw Millie and Sandra. "Welcome to 'The O'Grady's Ranch.' I'm ever so happy that your father has gotten this job working with our horses. Now we can go riding together, Sandra."

"I'm pleased, too, Sammie," exclaimed Sandra.

"Come on, girls, I'll show you all around the ranch."

Lester then told Ryan about his pay. "Oh, that's a lot, Lester. I never expected to be paid that much."

He then handed Ryan the address to the house that they would be living in. "Also, Ryan, you will receive a beginning bonus. We want anyone who works for the O'Grady's to dress well, which includes your daughters and your wife."

"I can't wait to tell my wife about everything that's happened today."

Sandra and Sammie became friends. Sandra was later invited often to the mansion house to play with Sammie and her friends.

Chapter Twenty-Three

Grandpa O'Grady

Sammie was ever so glad that she was able to find a way to help the Cunningham family. Sammie did get to go with Mrs. Cunningham and her girls as they shopped for all their new clothes. They were all in 7th heaven for sure.

Ryan was doing so well with his new job. He loved working with horses again. He was happy that his wife and daughters were pleased with their house and were grateful for the O'Grady's providing a beginning bonus, which allowed them to get new clothes and all the new furniture for their home.

Summer was drawing to an end, and school would be starting. Some of the kids had heard that Sandra and Millie's father was now working for the O'Grady's, and we're doing well financially.

On the first day of school, most of the kids couldn't believe how nicely Sandra and Millie were dressed. There was no more teasing from their classmates.

A lot of the boys saw how pretty Sandra was now with her hair done up so nice. She dressed better than most of her classmates. She had lots of kids buzzing around her.

Amy was in high school now. Sammie was sure missing her. Amy got rides to school from some of the new friends.

Her brother, Logan, had graduated from high school and decided not to go to college, which displeased his parents. Logan wanted to stay on at the ranch and work. He also loved helping on the farm by his house. Logan had been doing this since he was about ten years old and was hoping maybe to get promoted to something on the ranch.

Sammie, Rebecca, Rachel, and Jennifer could hardly wait to enter high school this next year. She then could be with Amy a little more. Amy's little sister, Beverley, was ten years old now, and she was looking forward to going to middle school.

Simon and Hannah's little Kassie was now five and the cutest little girl ever. She would be going to kindergarten this year. Sammie's grandfather, Samuel, sure loved playing with Kassie.

The harvesting of the Valencia oranges was almost over, and the ranch's year was one of the best ever.

Samuel O'Grady's health wasn't getting any better, and he knew that his future was uncertain. He had appointed his son, Simon, and Melvin, his ranch foremen, and now Lester,

Kate's husband, to run the ranch. Everything seemed to be running very smoothly.

Samuel, however, was concerned about Kate and Lester and all the vast wealth they had acquired. He decided to call them in to talk about it. As they arrived, Samuel greeted them. "I've called you here today because I wanted to know what you were thinking about your future. With all the wealth you've acquired, it's hard not to think about all the things that you could be doing with it."

Kate then responded, "Samuel, you'll never know what a battle Lester and I have been having with that question of yours. I know you would prefer that we stay here on the ranch. I know you're also counting on Sammie wanting to stay and help manage the ranch after she finishes her college. I think she will, Samuel. She loves this ranch."

"Again, Kate, what about your newfound wealth, and what have you planned for your future together?"

"Well, I'd like to put a lot of money into upgrading the ranch in all areas, and maybe even adding new things," Kate explained. She then added, "What do you think about our helping you expand your ranch with new things?"

"Am I hearing that you *do* want to stay here on the ranch, Kate?"

"Yes, and no, Samuel. We want to do some other things, like open some other small businesses. We would, however, oversee those who would be running those businesses. The ranch would be our main concern."

That seemed to satisfy Samuel for the present.

It was December, and another busy season for harvesting was upon them. The oranges, grapefruit, and tangerines were being harvested. Christmas vacation was just a few days away, and Amy, Beverly, and Sammie promise to help a little with the harvesting.

It was a great Christmas this year. Kate and Lester just weren't sure how much to spend on Sammie, because the sky was the limit. They did make her Christmas a little better and didn't get too crazy with gifts.

Spring had now arrived, and they were finishing the picking of the grapefruit and Cara Cara Oranges. It was time to harvest the Valencia Oranges next.

It was early April, and Sadie was looking for Samuel, her husband. She thought, "I'm sure he's in his office or on the patio."

As she entered his office, she saw him in his chair, slumped over on his desk. Sadie yelled, "Maria, Justine, Doris, Joseph, come here!"

She found that he was breathing. Joseph was the first to come. "Oh, my Sadie, I'll call 911."

When the ambulance came, they found that Samuel had passed away. By now, Simon, Hannah, Kate, Lester, Logan, Melvin, Letta, and others were there to comfort Sadie. The girls were all in school and didn't know what had happened yet.

Amy was the first one to come home. Her high school friends had dropped her off. She was shocked at the news of Samuel's passing. Soon the other girls were dropped off by their school bus driver, Bob.

Sammie, Amy, and Beverly were so very sad and hugged Sadie over and over again, crying with her.

It was the next day, and Sadie called Simon and Hannah to her. "Simon, I need you and Hannah close to me now. I want you to move here to the mansion to be with me. I'll need you both now more than ever."

Hannah then responded, "Mother, Simon, and I would be happy to be here with you, right, Simon?"

"Yes, Mother. What will we do with our house then? Oh, I know, Kate and Lester can move there while their mansion is being completed."

"No, Simon. I want you and Hannah and Kate and Lester here. I really do need you *all* supporting me now. Please do this for me!"

Simon then spoke, "I hate leaving my house vacant. I wish I could think of who might enjoy living there, but I don't know who."

Sadie then suggested, "Simon, what about Melvin and his family?"

"No, mother, Melvin needs to stay close to our Mexican families. He's what makes our ranch a success."

Hannah then added, "What about that new family, the Cunningham's. It would be better to have them closer, instead of being down in town, and then our house wouldn't be vacant."

"Wow, Hannah. That would be like going from night to day for them. Let me think about that."

Three days had passed, and Simon didn't know if the Cunningham's were really ready for such a profound change of going from a mediocre life to a very wealthy atmosphere and living in the mini-mansion.

Simon finally made his decision. He would go up to the stables and see Ryan Cunningham.

As Simon arrived, he saw Ryan brushing one of the horses. "Hello, Mr. O'Grady."

"Ryan, please call me Simon. You are one of the O'Grady's families now. I hope you will feel that way."

"I'm beginning to Mr. O'Grady, oh, I mean, Simon," Ryan laughed.

"Ryan, I know that you and your family have been overwhelmed with all the changes that have happened to you all so quickly."

"We're ever so happy and so blessed," commented Ryan. "Our family thanks you for all you O'Grady's have done for us."

"Are you ready for another big change, Ryan?"

"I don't know what other wonderful things you could possibly do for us, Simon."

"Since my father has passed away, my mother wants me and my family to move to the big mansion house. She also requested that Lester and Kate stay with her there as well."

"I hope you're not suggesting that my family move into *your* house, Simon."

"Yes, Ryan, that's exactly what I'm telling you. We don't want it standing empty."

"I don't know what to say. We love the big house that you are letting us use rent-free. What will people think about us living in such luxury on the O'Grady property?"

"As I said, Ryan, you're considered to be one of us now. You may start moving in anytime you wish. All the furnishing in our smaller mansion house will be left there for your use. You may change anything you like to make it feel more like your own home."

Simon then left, hoping that he did the right thing.

Ryan then ran to call his wife with the news. She screamed, not believing what she had just heard her husband say.

The news was soon all over the area. People just couldn't believe that the Cunningham's could be that fortunate.

Chapter Twenty-Four

Millie's Birthday Party

The Cunningham's began to move into the mini-mansion. Of course, Sammie was there trying to be of help. Sandra and Sammie were becoming best friends. Rebecca, Rachel, and Jennifer were becoming a little jealous.

As the Cunningham's were moving in, Ryan's wife said, "Ryan, what are we going to do with all the new furniture that we have just purchased for the other house?"

"Well, since this mansion has furniture already, Francis, and it's much better than what we have just purchased, I'm not sure. I'll ask Simon what he thinks we should do."

Millie was just entering the second grade, and the kids in her class were happy that she was dressing so much better now. She loved having everything be better than it use to be.

Millie's birthday was coming up in two weeks. She went to her father and asked, "Dad, my birthday is in two weeks. Could I please have a party, please?"

Sandra and Sammie were standing near-by, helping Sandra's dad. "Father, let her have her birthday here in the mini-mansion," pleaded her big sister.

Sammie then added, "Sandra, after my mother inherited all that money, the kids in school started treating me so different. They made some terrible comments. I'm wondering if Millie did invite some kids from her class if they would come?"

"Oh, Sammie, you're right. That could happen to Millie."

Then Millie shouted, "That wouldn't happen to me, Sammie!" She then turned to her Dad again and declared, "Daddy, I still want to have a party!"

"Millie, even if *none* of those kids from your school come, you'd still have a great party," her Dad related. He continued, "There would be Beverly, Amy, Logan, and her parents. There would be Kassie O'Grady and her parents, Simon and Hannah. And don't forget Sammie, Kate, Lester plus Sadie. Now, that's a lot of people!"

"How many people is that, Dad?"

Sammie broke in and said, "That's about fourteen, Millie, also including Sandra and your parents."

"Dad," commented Sandra, "Sammie, Amy, and I will prepare everything for Millie's party."

"I'm still going to invite my whole class," cried Millie. So be prepared for them too. I know my class will come."

School had started, and everyone was treating Millie as she hoped they would. The next day she passed out invitations to her upcoming party. It said that all parents were welcome to come as well.

One of Millie's friends, Kara Lynn, said, "I heard some kids saying they wouldn't come." That made Millie sad.

The day finally arrived, and Millie was now wondering whether any of the kids would come. The time for the party to start was 5:00 p.m. At 4:45 p.m., she saw a bunch of cars coming, and they keep coming.

Many, if not all, of her class, was there. She was so happy! Kara Lynn told Millie that the ones who said they weren't coming were made to go by their parents.

The children's parents were very curious about the Cunningham's good fortune.

Ryan and Francis Cunningham were delighted to become better acquainted with the neighbors that previously had not been so friendly.

Millie was thrilled for sure about her party being a success.

Sandra then commented to Sammie and Amy, "Well, we did it! I'm glad we made the extra food. I was sure that most of it was going to be wasted. When my birthday comes up in January, I think I'd be afraid to do what Millie did."

Sammie then added, "I just did the unexpected with my thirteenth birthday, Sandra, and had a wonderful party at Rebecca's house, right, Amy?"

"Yes, and I was surprised that it went so well," Amy responded.

"Sandra,... Rebecca, Amy, and I will help you plan your next birthday," said Sammie. We'll figure out something really fun to do for your birthday."

Millie then thanked Amy, Sammie, and her sister, Sandra, for making her party a success and then remarked, "Now that I'm eight years old, I don't want to be called Millie anymore. That's a baby name, and some of the kids at school tease me with my name being Millie. I want to be called *Melissa*, which is my real name. I'm going to tell my Mom, Dad, my teacher, and all my friends to call me *Melissa*, from now on."

Millie, oh, I mean, Melissa, my real name is Samantha, but I like my nickname, Sammie. I do see why you'd rather be called Melissa though. I do like it better."

"Thanks," Sammie," replied Melissa.

Chapter Twenty-Five

Money, Money

The Cunninghams were getting settled in the mini-mansion and were now being accepted more in the surrounding community. Simon and Hannah O'Grady missed their mini-mansion, but they were learning to live in the big mansion with Kate, Lester, Sammie, and Simon's mother.

Sadie, Kate, Hannah, and Letta went to the mini-mansion to welcome Francis Cunningham to the ranch. When they arrived, Sadie addressed Francis, "We truly do hope you'll feel a part of this ranch, and love being here with us all."

"Yes," added Kate, "We'll plan on getting together every so often so we can know you even better."

Late one night, when Lester came home to the big mansion, he found Kate, his wife, reading in their bedroom.

"You look tired, Lester."

"Yes, Kate, my day was a busy one for sure."

"I have some news, Lester. I got a telegram at about 3:00 p.m. today."

"Oh, no, Kate, is it about your mother?"

"Yes, Lester. She passed away late this morning. Her lawyers want to meet with us two days after the funeral. I haven't any idea how much everything she had is worth."

"Kate, her significant estate with its beautiful grounds will soon be in shambles unless it's kept up. Just by itself alone, the estate must be worth millions."

Kate called her mother's lawyers to be sure that the gardeners stayed on the job to keep the property in excellent shape. She also asked the household staff to stay on as well.

After the funeral, which was nice, but not too well attended, Kate and Lester went to the estate. The staff had prepared a very lovely luncheon for those who had attended the funeral.

Kate and Lester decided to stay on at the estate for a few days and asked the lawyers to have the meeting at the Stewart mansion.

The day came, and the lawyers came to give Kate and Lester the news of what they would be inheriting.

They were informed that the estate would sell for about forty-two million, maybe much more. Her mother's stocks, bonds, and five other businesses she owned were worth an estimated at sixty-eight million dollars, for a total of about one hundred ten million dollars.

After the lawyers had departed, Lester remarked, "Let's stay here at our estate for a few more days. Let's let Sammie invite whatever friends she would like to come here for a few days."

"I don't know, Lester. You're needed back at the ranch."

"Kate, we have money, money, money. Don't you want to enjoy some of it?"

"Lester, I grew up in this house. It has a lot of bad memories for me. I just want to sell it and move on with my life. We'll build our own estate with a big mansion on it, but it will be ours."

Kate reluctantly agreed to stay a few more days.

When Sammie heard that she could bring some of her friends to the Stewart Estate, she cheered, "I'm going to call all my close friends." She did, and there were Amy, Beverly, Rebecca, Rachel, and Jennifer. Jennifer's mother came with the girls.

Kate was surprised that their teachers agreed to let them take a few days off from school.

Sammie's mother ordered a limousine to pick up Sammie's friends at the airport. Sammie and Lester were there when they got off the plane. There were lots of hugs.

When her friends arrived at the vast estate after their flight, they were all so very impressed. They couldn't believe how beautiful the grounds were kept and how elegant the mansion was.

Kate welcomed Sammie's friends, and Jennifer's mother, "Did you all enjoy your flights?"

"Yes," they all exclaimed.

"Thank you, Clare, for coming with the girls."

"I was happy to help. This estate sure is big and so beautiful."

"Mom, let's live here. It's all yours, right?"

"Yes, Sammie, it's all mine, but won't you miss your Grandmother and your friends. You already live in a mansion."

"Yes, but this one is so much better. It's unbelievable. It's wonderful. I hope the one that you're building will be this great, Mom."

The girls all had a wonderful time with events that had been planned for them. Soon they flew home. Lester just didn't want to leave yet."

"Lester, I know you love this place, but think about me. I hate this place. Now I'm booking a plane ticket for tomorrow. Are you coming with me?"

"Yes, Kate, I'm coming back with you. I'm sorry for the way I've been acting, but I've been enjoying this place."

Kate was beginning to worry about Lester. She was sure that he was thinking about all the things he'd like to do with the money they had. They returned to the citrus ranch, and Kate thought that everything was returning to normal.

One evening after everyone was retiring, Sammie headed to her parent's room to say goodnight. She heard them arguing.

"Lester, money for some people can ruin their lives."

"Kate, why should I have to work so hard? I know that they pay me well, but we don't even need my pay. It seems so silly to be working when we have so much money. We or I could be doing some exciting things with that money."

"So, you don't like working here on the Ranch?"

"It's okay, Kate, but think about what we could be doing. We could be traveling the world. I've never even been out of Florida before except for going to North Carolina. Here I am, a millionaire, and stuck in a job that's just a job most anyone can do."

"Lester, we can plan some trips where ever you'd like to go. Lester, my family, and my close friends are *important* to me. We don't have to have a limit with having some fun with our wealth."

"Let's go to bed, Kate, I'm tired."

Just then, Sammie entered. "I heard what you both were arguing about. Lester, my mom is right; family and friends are *everythin*g!"

"I know, Sammie, you're right." He then kissed her goodnight.

She then ran over to her mother, and with hugs and kisses, she left.

Chapter Twenty-Six

Sammie's Ideas

Sammie had turned fourteen, and hopefully, a fun summer was in store for her. She was so looking forward to this fall as well, when she would be entering Harrison High School, which was in Melbourne, Florida. It was a little more than a half-hour drive. Sammie was so glad that Jennifer, Rachel, and Rebecca were still her best friends after all these years.

After dinner, one evening, Lester and her mother asked Sammie to come to the family room.

"So, what's this meeting for anyway? Am I in trouble for something I did?"

"No, Sammie," her mother began. "As you know, Lester and I have been trying to decide what to do with our money. We just finally found out that after the lawyers had sold everything, we will be getting is far more than the lawyers had told us we would get from my mother's estate."

"How much more, Mother?"

"They said we would get one hundred ten million, but we received thirty-six million more, for a total of one hundred and forty-six million."

"Wow! Mother, what will you do with all that money?"

"That's only part of the problem, Sammie. Every year we will add millions more to what we already have by getting interest on this money, or from investments, we may be making."

"I know what we can do with just a small part of this money. We've talked about this a little already. I'd like to modernize this citrus ranch completely."

Lester then asked, "What would you do to accomplish this, Sammie?"

"I would replace the sables and make them much larger. I would like to see more thoroughbred horses on the ranch. Also, I would like it to be the second place for horse shows here in Florida."

"That sounds great, Sammie," commented Lester. "I've always thought about doing something more with the stables, but I thought it would just cost too much. This now certainly is not the problem. I'm also going to check into these horse shows with the people who run them here in Florida. Sammie, that is an excellent thing to do with some of our money."

"Lester, we'll need to have a meeting with Simon and Hannah about this. He's part-owner of the ranch too," Kate expressed.

"Yes, you're right, Kate. I'll set up a meeting with Simon, Hannah, you and me."

"Wait a minute; I'm part owner in this ranch. I want to be at this meeting too." After all, it was my idea. I also have more to say about improvements here on the ranch," added Sammie."

"Sorry, Sammie, I thought you were through. What else would you change?" asked her mother.

"Well, I'd build a much better house for the Robinson's. Melvin and Letta have served this ranch so faithfully for a long time. Amy, Beverly, and Logan, I'm sure, would also like a lovely new modern house for them all to live in for many years. Indeed, not a mansion, they wouldn't expect that. I also think that grandma's mansion should be updated as well."

"Wait a minute, Sammie, you're right! The Cunningham's just moved into the mini-mansion. How do you think that made the Robinson's feel about that after their long years here?" exclaimed Kate.

"Kate, Simon has talked with both Melvin and Letta about that, and they know they must stay close to the Mexican families and the pickers who come in," explained Lester.

"One more thing now," Sammie interrupted. "I would make some new modern housing for the Mexican families who live here all the time. Replace those old barracks with some new ones. Maybe add a couple of other smaller houses for some guest pickers with families. Lester, with these new improvements, these pickers will want to come here more than other places if we make them more comfortable."

"Sammie, these are great ideas. We do have a problem with having enough pickers at times, that's for sure. If the word gets around, they will want to come here."

Kate then added. "We could add a beautiful swimming pool and a park for them as well. Let's spend some of this money!"

Lester then set up a meeting with Simon and Hannah. They informed them about all that they would like to do to improve the ranch. Simon was delighted with their ideas.

Kate said she would move about fifty million dollars over to the O'Grady Citrus Ranch checking accounts. She had a power of attorney to act for Sammie since Sammie wasn't eighteen yet.

Kate then spoke, "Lester and I are also setting up a charitable foundation to supply high school kids with scholarships that have at least a 3.0-grade average but wouldn't have the money to go to college. These scholarships would be for twelve different high schools in this area, at least for now."

Summer was over, and Sammie would soon be entering high school with her friends. The high schools in the area were thrilled about the news of scholarships for their students. Some students began to apply themselves even more to their studies so that they would qualify.

Chapter Twenty-Seven

Sammie Helping Others

Fall had finally arrived, and it was time to start school. After a few weeks had passed, Sammie was beginning to love Harrison High School. She was glad that Amy's friend, Cheryl, was giving her and Rebecca rides to school. Her other friends found rides with other kids.

Sammie had some classes with Rebecca, Rachel, and Jennifer. One afternoon while Sammie and her friends were going to their last class, two boys stopped them.

One of the boys asked, "Which one of you is Sammie?"

Sammie responded, "I am."

"I'm Jessie, and this is my friend, Bud. I heard all about your mother giving a lot of the smart kids in the area scholarships to colleges of their choice."

"That's right, Jessie."

"Why do only the smart college-bound kids get help, but never people like Bud and me who aren't cut out for college?

I guess things will never change," he exclaimed in disgust, and then they both left.

"You know, Sammie, he's right. I think you should tell your mother about what just happened here," expressed Jennifer.

"I never thought about this backfiring. I hope we can do something for other kids who want to do something more with their lives too. So many kids don't go to college," declared Sammie. "When I get home, I'm going to talk to my mother about this, girls."

As Sammie arrived at the mansion, she went looking for her mother. Rufus, their dog, was always there waiting for Sammie to come home after school.

She headed for the kitchen. Maria always knew where everyone was.

"Maria, where's my mom?"

"She went to Orlando with your step-dad. They said they would be returning later this evening."

"Oh, I wanted to talk to them about what happened at school today."

"I hope it wasn't anything terrible, Sammie."

"No, but it's something we can do to help kids at the high schools."

Sammie went on to explain to Maria what had happened at her school. "Sammie, this boy, Jessie, is right. I bet your mother will find a way to help those kids too," Maria declared.

Her mother and step-father didn't get home until about 9:30 p.m. Sammie then explained what happened at school.

"Sammie, I guess I never thought about the other kids. We can pay for the kids to go to a vocational school. They offer many kinds of jobs that will pay much more than working for retail stores and fast food places. Some of these kinds of schools also add getting apprenticeships for many trades, such as plumbers, electricians, construction workers, and so many more. If any of the kids want to be police officers and firemen, they can by applying in the cities where they live for these jobs which are not offered as part of the vocational school's programs."

"Mom, what about the girls and the jobs they can do?"

"There are lots of jobs they can learn from being trained in vocational schools, such as Dental Hygienist, Medical Sonographer, Registered Nurse, Web Developer, and so many more."

"How soon can you get this going, Mom?"

"Sammie, school is just in its first few weeks. Lester and I will visit several vocational schools in the coming days, and we'll begin to investigate programs that high school graduates can apply for at various vocational schools in the state of Florida."

"Mom, can I tell kids in school that you're putting this together, and that it will be ready by the end of this school year?"

"I guess it will be okay, Sammie. I don't know for sure how this will all work, though, but in the end, it will be free for kids who are serious about wanting to better their lives."

The next day at school, Sammie saw Jessie. She called to him. "Jessie, Jessie!"

He stopped and said, "What do you want, rich girl?"

"Thank you so much, Jessie, for waking me up to the needs of the other kids who won't be going to college for various reasons. I talked to my mother, and she's going to be setting up free tuition at vocational schools for high school graduates. They offer many types of jobs that pay very well. Some of the schools last only a few months; others may be up to two years."

"Your mother can do that for us kids?"

"Yes, Jessie, she can."

"Can I tell other kids about this?" cried Jessie.

"Yes, my Mom said it would be okay to talk about it around our school. It won't be public knowledge for a while, though.

She promised it would be ready by the end of this school year for high school graduates."

The school principal couldn't believe the rumor that was flying all around the school. She called Sammie into her office. "Sammie, is it true that kids will have free tuition for any trade school?"

"Yes, Mrs. Carlson, it's true. My mother will be working with several vocational schools over the next few weeks setting everything up. It's just for the same twelve high schools that will get these free scholarships."

The principal started calling several other high schools with this new announcement about the vocational school's free tuition for high school graduates.

Chapter Twenty-Eight

Many Changes in the Ranch

All the kids in Sammie's high school were so excited about the news of the O'Grady's helping so many kids in many of the local high schools. The kids began thinking of the great things that they could do with more education.

Sammie was a very popular girl in her school! At lunchtime, Rebecca, Jennifer, Rachel, and Sammie were eating their lunches together.

"I can't believe all the activities that are going on at the ranch," cried Sammie. "I had a meeting just a couple of weeks ago with my parents, suggesting things that they could do on the ranch, and they're doing it!"

"Like what kind of things?" Jennifer inquired.

"New stables, with lots more horses, and maybe creating an arena that could possibly be the second place to have horse shows in our state."

Rebecca asked, "You said you might get a new horse."

"Yes, I'm looking for just the right thoroughbred horse."

"I heard that your new house, or is it a mansion, is going up pretty fast. When will it be done?" Jennifer wanted to know.

"Oh, I'm not sure, Jennifer. It could take up to six to nine months and maybe a lot longer. They have major work to do on the land that surrounds the mansion. They will make it look beautiful, like my grandmother's wonderful gardens that are around her mansion."

Sammie continued, "My friend Amy and her family are getting a much larger house built for them too. They sure have made the O'Grady ranch a success," Sammie added.

"It's too bad that your picker's families have to live in their old places. I've seen those barracks too. They're not very nice!" cried Rebecca.

"Rebecca, they're a lot nicer than others around the state. I was just going to tell you about that. The families who live here will have some fine smaller homes built for them, and there will be parks for their kids to play in, plus a big swimming pool. You mentioned the barracks. They will be torn down, and all-new barracks will be built for the single pickers. If some of the guest pickers have families, we'll have some new smaller homes for them too."

"Wow, Sammie. I think that's wonderful!" cried Jennifer.

Sammie then told her friends, "I'm going this Saturday with my Uncle Simon and Mr. Cunningham to pick out my new thorough breed horse. I'm inviting you, girls, to all come with me, please!"

They all said they would love to come. Saturday came, and the four girls all had different ideas of which horse was the best. Sammie finally decided to buy the one that her Uncle Simon told her was the best choice. Her three friends agreed that she had picked the right horse.

Late one evening, Sammie saw her Uncle Simon coming up the stairs in the mansion. "Uncle Simon, can I talk to you?"

"Yes, Sammie. Let's go back down to my office."

"Uncle Simon, it's sure nice to have you and Hannah living here in the big mansion now. I love playing with Kassie too."

"Tell me what's on your mind, Sammie."

"Well, Uncle Simon, its Lester. He seems so unhappy being tied down to working here on the ranch when he and my mother have hundreds of millions of dollars. He wants to start some new smaller businesses that he can oversee. He also wants to travel the world."

"Yes, Sammie, I've got that message from the little comments he makes. I'm not sure what to do."

"What if you hired another person to take his place and let him continue to work. Let him know you're aware that he wants to do other things like travel and have other interests. Tell him you understand and that he's free to do all these things, but just to let you know when they're planning on traveling and for how long. Let him know that he's a valuable part of the management team for the ranch and that you want him to stay on to help you."

"Sammie, you're so very wise. You've given me the answer I've been searching for so long. Now I know what to do to have peace and harmony on this ranch." He stood and hugged Sammie. "I love you, dear. This ranch will be a wonderful place when it's all done, and it's all because of you."

"Uncle Simon, I plan on helping you run the ranch after my college education is complete. I do love this place. I sure miss my grandpa, though, and again I'm glad you have agreed to come and live here in the mansion to help comfort my grandma."

Chapter Twenty-Nine

Sammie's High School Years

Sammie was enjoying her first year of high school. One day she saw a boy she had known since middle school.

"Hi, Alex, it's good to see you. I didn't know you were going to this school too. The last time I saw you, you told me you were moving out of Florida."

"Oh, that changed, Sammie. My dad got a better paying job here, and we decided to stay after all. I'm so happy to see you. I'm on my way to my math class now."

"I'm taking math this year as well, that's where I'm going too. Let's hurry, or we'll both be late."

"Sammie, after class, can I walk you to the lunchroom and join you and your friends?"

"Yes, Alex, we'd love to have you join us. I think you know Jennifer, Rachel, and Rebecca, right?"

"Yes, I do know them."

Alex had a terrible crush on Sammie since middle school, and now seeing her again, he was so glad to be around her again. Sammie was only fourteen, so she couldn't date yet, but Alex and Sammie became even better friends through their first year of high school.

Soon, the second year of high school started. Amy and her friend, Cheryl, who gave them rides to the high school, told Sammie that they would be staying after school to go to the cheerleading try-outs. Amy and Cheryl were both in their senior year now and had tried out for the cheerleader's team before, but didn't make it.

Sammie, Jennifer, Rachel, and Rebecca wanted to try out too. Alex told Sammie, "There are very few girls who make the team as sophomores, but I guess you and your friends could try out if you would like."

Amy didn't make it again. She was so disappointed, but her friend Cheryl did. Next, the juniors tried out, and finally, it was the sophomore's turn. To Sammie's surprise, Jennifer made the team. Sammie, Rachel, and Rebecca didn't but were glad for their friend, Jennifer, who did.

The head cheerleader told the girls who were there, "If you didn't make the team this time, come back next year because there are a lot of the cheerleaders who are seniors and they won't be back next year. So girls, practice, practice, and practice some more!"

Alex decided to try out for the football team but also was disappointed that he hadn't been chosen. He told Sammie that he was sure he would make the team next year. She was proud of Alex for trying.

The next day as Alex and Sammie were on the way to the lunchroom after their math class, Alex asked, "Sammie, there's a dance coming up in two weeks. Would you go with me?"

"Alex, I'm only fifteen, and my parents won't let me date until I'm sixteen."

"Sammie, my parents have been asked to chaperone this dance, of course, with other parents as well. Please ask your parents if you can come, please!"

"I will ask, Alex, but I don't think they will let me."

"What if I ask my mom to call your mom?"

"Yes, Alex, that might work!"

Later that evening, Alex's mother called Kate, Sammie's mother. Kate agreed to let Sammie attend her very first dance with Alex.

Both Alex and Sammie were so delighted.

"Mom, we need to go shopping. I need a beautiful dress for my first dance."

They decided to go to Orlando to shop for her dress. Sammie did find a gorgeous dress. She was so excited for Alex to see her in her new dress.

The day of the dance had arrived. That evening, Sammie's mother was helping her to look her best. Suddenly Sammie heard the doorbell.

"Mother, I'm not ready yet!"

"It's okay, dear. Finish up, and I'll entertain Alex for you until you're ready."

When Sammie came down the stairs, Alex declared, "Sammie, you look so unbelievably beautiful. I love your dress. I think you'll be the most beautiful girl at this dance tonight."

They both ran out the front door of the mansion holding hands. They were a great looking couple. They both jumped into Alex's parent's car.

"Hi, Mr. and Mrs. Kelly. Oh, and Mrs. Kelly, thanks so much for calling my mother, thus making it possible for Alex and me to go to the dance this evening."

Alex's mother then commented, "Sammie, you're welcome. You do look so beautiful this evening."

"Thank you, Mrs. Kelly."

The dress was extra special. It would be something Sammie would always remember. She was starting to like Alex.

A few days later, at school, Alex asked Sammie out again. This time it was to one of their school football games.

"My mother won't mind me going to the football games, Alex, but not just with you. It must be with our friends as a group."

"That's okay with me, Sammie, just so long as I can be with you," Alex laughed.

"I'm going with a few of my friends," cried Sammie, "I'll see you at the game. Look for me!"

It was getting close to the end of school, and there was another dance coming up, but Sammie's birthday wouldn't be for about four weeks. She knew Alex was hoping Sammie's mother would let her go since her birthday was so close to coming.

In the meantime, a boy named Bill saw Sammie in the hall, just leaving her locker. "Wait up, Sammie!" Bill was on the football team and popular in their school.

"Oh, hi, Bill."

"Sammie, there's a dance coming up. It's the last dance before prom. Will you go with me?"

It took Sammie by surprise. She didn't know what to say. Most girls would kill to go to a dance with Bill.

"Well?" Bill questioned her again.

"I'm not allowed to date until I'm sixteen, Bill."

"Sammie, I saw you at the last dance with Alex."

"Yes, I was Bill, but only because of Alex's parents being chaperones at that dance. I was surprised that my mother agreed to let me go."

"When will you turn sixteen?" he asked her.

"In about four weeks."

"I'm sure you can talk your mom into letting you go. You've lived almost all of your sixteen years, right?"

Just then, Alex walked up to them. "Hi, Sammie, Bill."

"I was just asking Sammie to the upcoming dance," Bill related.

"Well, Sammie, are you going to go with Bill?"

"I haven't given him an answer yet, Alex."

"Then, since you haven't given him an answer, I'm also asking you to go with me, Sammie."

"I can't give either of you an answer. I'll have to ask my mother if I can even go, not being sixteen yet. See you, guys."

When Sammie got home, she asked her mom about going to the dance.

Her mother smiled and replied, "Of course, you may, my darling girl. You're almost sixteen, how could I ever deny you going?" She then hugged her.

"Mom, I have a problem. Two boys asked me to the dance. I told them I would first have to ask you if I could go."

"Who are the two boys? I guess one would be Alex, right, Sammie?"

"Yes, Mom, but Bill asked me first, and then Alex came along and found that Bill was asking me out to the dance. It was so awkward, Mom."

"So, who will you go with?"

"Alex, of course, in fact, I'm going up to call him right now!"

Alex and Sammie did go to that dance and also later to the prom. Sammie's prom was extra special for her now that she was almost sixteen.

Her mother made her sixteenth birthday special for her as well. Sammie invited both boys and girls. Her parents had an extra special gift for her. Sammie's birthday was on a Saturday. After her party was over and the kids were leaving, they saw Sammie's parents out in front of the mansion standing next to a new Ford Mustang convertible.

"Mother, Dad, is it really all mine!" she yelled.

"Yes, enjoy, Sammie. It is all yours," exclaimed her mother.

Sammie's friends were happy for her but were a little bit jealous that they couldn't be that lucky.

Soon it was summer. Alex, Sammie, and their friends all had a wonderful summer doing all kinds of fun things. Sammie loved her car. She was glad that she now had her own car to get to high school in Melbourne and would be able to have her friends ride with her.

Finally, it was Sammie's junior year. She tried out to be a cheerleader again and was accepted. She was in seventh heaven. Alex tried out for the football team and also made it.

Sammie and Alex were a very popular couple in their school, and this worried her parents. They wanted her to date others so she could compare different boys, but neither of them wanted to do that.

It was about the middle of the school year, and Jennifer and Sammie were loving being on the cheerleading team. Amy and her friend had graduated and were going to college in Orlando, Florida, so Sammie was glad that she had her own car now.

Football was in full swing in Sammie's school. During one of their games, as the cheerleaders were performing, Jennifer collapsed. She was rushed to the hospital. After two days, they still didn't know what was wrong with her. She was getting worse. She finally started recovering after almost a month of being in the hospital. The doctors never did find out what caused her to collapse. Everyone was so happy to see her finally go home. She was advised by her doctors that she couldn't go back to school for at least three to four weeks. All the kids were wondering if she could move on to her senior year or not.

Jennifer worked very hard to catch up with her studies, and she did. She now could be a senior when school started again, but she was not well enough to be on the cheerleading team. That was a huge disappointment to her.

The senior year finally arrived, and Sammie and Alex were looking at colleges and universities where they might want to go.

Sammie's senior year was great. She loved being a cheerleader and dating Alex, who was one of the stars of the football team. Their senior year couldn't have been any better. They both enjoyed their senior prom. It was the best ever.

Many of the students who were graduating appreciated getting a scholarship and also being able to pick a college of their choice. All of their tuition and other expenses would also be paid for them. Likewise, other kids not wanting to go to college picked specific jobs in the vocational schools.

Alex found a college that would give him a football scholarship. It was Michigan State, and that's where he decided to go. He called Sammie to tell her.

"Sammie, I got an excellent football scholarship at Michigan State! You'll love Michigan; I know you will."

"Alex, I decided to go to Florida State. I want to be close to my family and help around the ranch as much as I can. Rebecca will be going Florida State too; in fact, we'll be roommates with four other girls."

"Sammie, I know you were looking there, and I also looked at Florida State, but they weren't offering any football scholarships there."

"I'm sorry, Alex, but I'm going to go to Florida State. Football isn't everything. I'm very wealthy now that I turned eighteen, and I'm heir to all that my mother has. I'll be a billion-dollar heiress someday, and I was hoping you'd be at my side. Don't you want to marry me?"

"Well, Sammie, I can still marry you after I finish college. We just won't be seeing each other much. You're rich! You could fly to Michigan every couple of weeks, right?"

"Possibly, Alex."

After summer was over, Sammie did go to Florida State, and Alex went to Michigan State. Alex was always calling Sammie, but she was backing away from him little by little.

Chapter Thirty

What's Next for Sammie?

Sammie had a heavy load of classes for her first semester at Florida State College. She began wondering if taking on too much was going to be okay. Sammie knew her grades in high school were pretty good. She was going home most weekends. She missed everyone so much at the ranch.

Sammie was being asked out on dates by many guys, and she had turned them all down. She knew almost all of them probably had heard of her being very wealthy. She didn't want any guy dating her for her money.

On Friday after her last class, Rebecca and Sammie headed home. She still loved the car that she had received on her sixteenth birthday.

On their way home, Rebecca commented, "Sammie, I won't be going home with you on the weekends very much. I've got guys asking me for dates, and it's usually on Friday, Saturday, and even sometimes on Sunday too."

"That's fine, Rebecca, but it sounds like a lot of dating might be too much. When will you ever do your homework?"

"I know I can keep up. There's one guy whose name is Allen. Sammie, I really like him."

"Don't get too serious. Most of us want to finish college and then think about marriage."

"I know, Sammie, you're right, of course."

When Sammie reached home and entered the big mansion, she met her grandma. "Good to see you, Sammie. I'm so pleased that you've decided to come home most weekends."

"Grandma, how are you feeling?"

"Oh, I'm fine, my dear," her grandma replied.

"Now, Grandma, tell me the truth. How are you really feeling?" Sammie inquired again.

"I think a little better, but I'm going to miss you and your parents so much when you move into your new, much larger mansion."

"Oh, Grandma, I don't think it's bigger. It sure is taking so much more time than they expected. The grounds around our new mansion are starting to look so beautiful. I also think my mother is hiring too many servants. She has one for every little job around the mansion."

"Sammie, she'll learn quick enough what works and what does not."

"Grandma, in just the first couple of weeks at my college, I've had so many guys asking me out on dates."

"That's because you're so beautiful, Sammie," remarked her grandma.

"Maybe, but it's more than that, Grandma. It's because these guys know about how wealthy I am."

Sammie then asked, "Grandma, does my Uncle Simon happen to be home now?"

"Yes, Sammie, I saw him go into his office just before you arrived."

As she left, she shouted, "Love you, Grandma! See you at dinner."

As she approached her Uncle Simon's office and entered, he looked up and said, "Sammie, I am glad you came home this weekend. We sure miss not having you around as much."

"Uncle Simon, I need to talk to you about something."

"Come in and sit down. Is everything okay at school?"

"Well, that's what I want to talk to you about, Uncle Simon. I'm getting a bunch of guys asking me out. I'm pretty sure it's because they know about my wealth. I don't know what to do?"

"Have you accepted any dates yet, Sammie?"

"No, Uncle, I haven't, but they keep coming back and asking again."

"What about Alex, your boyfriend, Sammie?"

"Oh, he's busy with school at Michigan State. He thinks football is more important than being with me. I've been backing away from him, Uncle Simon."

She continued, "I'm thinking about going to a college far from the United States where no one would know about me. I want to get my college education finished and return here to work with you and Lester."

"Sammie, you'll have to finish the semester you're in now before you can make a move to a new college. Let me think about what I can do about this problem of yours, okay?"

After dinner, Sammie hurried up to her room to study. Early Monday morning, she drove over to get Rebecca.

When she got there, Rebecca asked, "Well, did you tell your family about your problems, Sammie?"

"Yes, I talked to my Uncle Simon about maybe going to another college that would be out of the United States."

"You can't leave me, Sammie!"

"Rebecca, I see that you've been making friends with some of our roommates, and you *did* say you would be dating a lot."

"Yes, I have enjoyed making new friends with our new roommates. I guess I will be dating more too. Sammie, I just got a great idea to keep these guys away from you. Buy a diamond ring, and when a guy asks for a date, just hold your hand out and say, 'Sorry, I'm engaged,'" laughed Rebecca.

"You know, Rebecca, that does sound like a good idea. I'll be giving that some thought," she smiled.

As the weeks passed, Alex's calls from Michigan became less and less. He was angry at Sammie for not agreeing to fly to Michigan to see him. Soon they both decided to call it quits. Sometimes first loves don't last.

As the school semester ended, Sammie collected up all of her things and headed home. This time she went to her parent's new mansion. It was finished after all these months of waiting. It was big, and the grounds were unbelievably beautiful. Sammie's parents started traveling a lot, so the estate was empty except for all the servants her mother had hired.

Sammie's Uncle Simon took his pickup truck over to Sammie's parent's new mansion. Simon knew her parents were away somewhere in London. He didn't knock; he just entered and called, "Sammie, where are you? It's your Uncle Simon."

One of the housekeepers came up to him and said, "She's up in her room, unpacking her school things, Mr. O'Grady."

He went up the big staircase and entered her room. "Well, how do you like your new home?"

"It's pretty nice, but I miss everyone over at the main mansion for sure. How's my grandma doing, Uncle Simon?"

"Not well at all, Sammie. I'm apprehensive about her health. She's just not taking very good care of herself. She also won't listen to her doctors."

"So, what did you find out about another college?"

"I don't think you have to leave the United States, Sammie. There are a lot of wonderful small colleges where you can obtain your degree."

"Really! Tell me what you've found out so far?" she asked her uncle.

"Let's go downstairs and sit in your library. Sammie, I found two great colleges in Oregon. One is in Salem and is called Corban University. The other one I found is the one I hope you may consider. It's Linfield College, and it's in the small town of Mc Minnville, Oregon. It only has about 35,000 people. It's located in the northwest part of Oregon and is famous for the many vineyards around that part of the country. It's in a beautiful part of Oregon, Sammie."

"Will you take me to visit this Linfield College, Uncle Simon?"

"Yes, I'd love to take you to see it. We'll leave this next Wednesday. We'll fly there in our family jet. We could fly into McMinnville with our private plane, but we don't want to announce that you're from a wealthy family, right? We'll rent a car in Portland and drive to McMinnville. It's about an hour and twenty-minute drive from Portland."

"That sounds fine, Uncle. I think I would like a college in a smaller town better."

They went, and Sammie loved everything about the college. The area was so breathtakingly beautiful. She signed up for the second semester. Simon and Sammie then returned to Florida.

Sammie only had a few days, and the second semester would be starting. She was sad knowing she would be so far from the ranch she loved so very much. Sammie also worried about her grandma. It was time to leave. She headed over to the main mansion. Everyone was there to say their good-byes.

Simon then took her to the airport. "We'll miss you, Sammie."

She was finally on her way, looking for a new adventure in her life. She had only been at her new college for about three weeks when she got a call from her mother.

"Sammie, your grandmother has just passed away. Please come home. The funeral will be in four days."

"I'll fly home tomorrow, Mom. I'm so glad you weren't away on vacation somewhere far away."

There were a lot of people who came to the funeral. The church was packed. Sammie cried and cried. Now both of her grandparents were gone. She remembered how she could always go to them with her problems, especially her grandfather.

Simon and Hannah were now the only ones living in the main mansion with just their daughter, Kassie.

Kate and Lester were now in their own new mansion, and, of course, Sammie when she would come home at various times.

"Things were now going to seem different with my grandparents gone," Sammie thought.

Chapter Thirty-One

Will All of Sammie's Dreams Come True?

After the funeral, Sammie returned to her college. No guys had asked her out yet. The students were friendly and kind, and she loved her professors. She knew she had made the right decision going to this small college.

After a few weeks into her second semester, a guy name Chester asked her for a date to go to the movies in town. She accepted and enjoyed the time she had with Chester.

It was two weeks later, and Chester hadn't called her for another date. "Maybe he didn't like me," she thought.

A few days later, a student bumped into Sammie as she was coming out of the college book store, causing her to drop all of her books.

"Oh, I'm so sorry. Let me help you pick up your books." After they had finished collecting everything, he said, "I'm Benjamin. I'm new to this college. I went to another one in Portland for my first semester, but I didn't like it. No one was friendly like this college. I love it here."

"That's just what happened to me," cried Sammie, "I tried a big university and left for this small-town college, and like you, Benjamin, I'm so enjoying everything about this college."

Benjamin then inquired, "What's your name?"

"I'm Sammie. I'm from Florida. My parents work on a farm there."

"My parents live in Portland. My dad drives a truck for an auto parts place. My mom works as a waitress in a fancy restaurant. The college in Portland was too expensive and not friendly as I have already told you, so I looked for a small-town college. Linfield College was the cheapest tuition that I could find."

Benjamin stopped talking and just stared at Sammie. "We sure seem to have a lot in common. I want to get to know you better, Sammie. Would you go with me to the basketball game on Friday?"

Sammie thought for a minute and replied, "I'd love to go with you, Benjamin."

As the month flew by, Sammie and Benjamin grew closer, and this was something that she had always dreamed of, someone to love her for who she was, and not because of her money. When would she ever find the right time to tell Benjamin the truth about her wealth?

Sammie was feeling so confused about Benjamin. Spring vacation was coming up, and she knew she would be flying home. She couldn't wait to tell her family at the ranch all about Benjamin, and how she was beginning to have feelings for him.

The night before she left Benjamin, he exclaimed, "I'm going to miss you so much. I don't have enough money to go home to Portland, and I always hate asking my parents for more money when they're trying so hard to keep me in this college. My part-time job at the cafeteria does help, though."

Sammie took a bus to Portland and then flew home on a commercial airline. Joseph usually would have been there to pick her up, but her Uncle Simon knew from the letters she wrote to her mother that she really needed to talk to him about her problems. He was hoping he could help comfort her.

As she got off the airplane, her Uncle Simon was there. "Hi, Sammie. How was your flight?"

"Fine," she answered him.

Neither of them said much until they got into Simon's car. "Your mother let me read your letters. I hope that was okay, Sammie."

"Yes, uncle, it's okay with me. I'm glad you came instead of Joseph."

"Tell me about Benjamin."

"Well, there are two things. First, I may be falling for Benjamin. Second, I haven't told him about my money. It was my plan, of course, not to let anyone know about my wealth, right, Uncle Simon?"

"Yes, Sammie, that was the plan, and the first part worked. I now see your concern about your having these feelings toward Benjamin and now trying to figure out what to do about it."

"Uncle Simon, how will I break the news to him that I'm wealthy?"

"Sammie, if Benjamin is *the one*, and you're sure, tell him, and more importantly, tell him why you didn't tell him. Tell him about your experiences at Florida State College, and all the guys that asked you out on dates because of your money. I'm sure he'll understand, and he will if he loves you."

"That sure sounds easy, Uncle Simon, but…"

"Don't make it harder than it needs to be. Like I said, just do it, Sammie. Take a deep breath and get it done."

Sammie's ten days at the ranch were great. She made the most of every day.

It was time to leave. Sammie and her uncle drove to Orlando. Simon, her uncle, decided again to take the family jet and fly to Portland. They had a pleasant flight and talked about just everything; it was great to be with her uncle. She did love him.

They finally landed in Portland, and Sammie got a rental car and drove the rest of the way to McMinnville, Oregon.

When she arrived back, there sat Benjamin in front of her dorm. "Benjamin, how long have you been sitting there?"

"Not that long. One of your roommates said you called and told her you'd be back on Friday about 5:00 p.m. or so."

Sammie ran to him. "I love you for being here for me when I got home, Benjamin!" she exclaimed, hugging him. "There is something I wanted to talk to you about," Sammie said hesitantly.

"Wait! There's something I want to tell you first!" exclaimed Benjamin. "Sammie, I love you so much, and I want to spend the rest of my life with you. Will you marry me?" He pulled out a small diamond ring. "We can be engaged as long as you want."

"I love you too!" Sammie exclaimed. "I would love to be engaged to you, Benjamin. I want to spend the rest of my life with you too!"

After they finished hugging and kissing, Benjamin said, "What were you going to tell me?"

Sammie hesitated. She was so scared that if she told Benjamin the truth that he might change his mind about her. "Oh, I just wanted to tell you how much I had missed you!" she said.

Soon afterward, they decided to set the wedding date. June 20th was the date they set for their wedding. It would take place in Portland. Sammie called her mother and told her about the time they both had chosen to be married. Sammie still had not told Benjamin about her being wealthy. How would she do it?

Chapter Thirty-Two

A New Beginning

It was May 15th, and Sammie's first year of college would be ending on the 28th of May. Sammie's birthday was coming up on the 23rd of May. She never told Benjamin when her birthday was. He never asked her, but she didn't know his birthday either.

Sammie's birthday had always been an amazing day for her, and now it probably wouldn't be. This made her sad the nearer her birthday got. Finals were starting on the very day of her birthday.

On the 22nd, Sammie and Benjamin had a date to see a movie. She planned to tell him about her money that very evening.

That evening as they headed to the movies, Benjamin spoke, "Sammie, my parents got a loan to help with our wedding costs. They didn't want to burden your parents with all the expenses. You know, flying to Florida and back will be expensive for my parents. They said their loan would be paid back in ten years. I'm sure proud of them for wanting to help us."

Sammie wanted so badly to tell him right then, but couldn't. After the movie, she had planned to tell him everything. Again she didn't.

Sammie always had everything she wanted, and tomorrow would be a terrible day for her. She felt awful that she was so selfish about this.

The next day was Friday, and she was to meet Benjamin at his dorm at 5:00 p.m. When she arrived and walked in, there were a whole lot of people there that she knew.

"Happy Birthday, Sammie!" Then to her surprise, her mother came up from behind the crowd of people that were there.

"Mother, I thought this would be the saddest day of my life. I wondered why you didn't call me this morning. I was really in the dumps for sure."

"Sammie, I called Benjamin and asked him if he knew it was your birthday on the 23rd of May. He told me that you hadn't said when your birthday was. Sammie, after he heard when your birthday was, he went into action and planned this neat party for you. I wanted to come here to meet your finance and help celebrate with you."

She went to Benjamin and hugged him. Sammie then went to her mother and pulled her away from the crowd. "Mother,

I haven't told Benjamin about our money. I sure hope you didn't say anything to him?"

"No, dear, I didn't. I think you had better do it right now," her mother strongly suggested.

"Right now, Mother, what about all my guests?"

"Sammie, right now!"

After she left her mother, she pulled Benjamin aside.

"Benjamin, I need to tell you something, and I hope you won't be displeased as to what I'm about to say to you."

"Oh, you mean about how wealthy you are? One of my friends brought me an article about your family this morning, and it told all about the O'Grady's and how your mother inherited over a billion dollars."

Sammie beat on Benjamin's chest, "You're mean! You should have called me this morning and told me how you feel about me being so wealthy. Are you disappointed in me for not telling you about this? And do you still love me, anyway?"

"Maybe I was a little disappointed for you not telling me. As to still loving you, my dearest Sammie, I do more than ever!" he laughed.

She then went on to tell him why she hadn't told him earlier about her wealth and about what happened at Florida State University with all the guys asking her out.

"Benjamin, I wanted someone to love me for me, and certainly not my money."

The next day Sammie went to the bank and paid off Benjamin's parent's loan and told Benjamin not to tell his parents.

"But, Sammie, when no envelope comes from the bank for their first payment, they'll call the bank. They'll know someone in your family paid it off."

"So, we're all family now. I'll also send them their tickets for coming to the reception in Florida. I've tried to find out about the other things they have paid for to make our wedding special as well, but didn't find any others."

The wedding in Portland was extra special. The wedding took place in Benjamin's church. They went to a nice restaurant afterward. His parents had done a great job of putting everything together for them.

A few days later, the reception in Florida was tremendous. There were a lot of people there. Sammie sure missed her grandparents not being there though.

After the reception, Sammie and Benjamin took a six-week honeymoon trip all over Europe. They saw many countries on their incredible journey. When they returned, they were ready to go to work on the ranch, at least for the rest of the summer. In September, they would be going to Florida State together. They both knew they would be missing their other college, which they loved so much.

Benjamin was having a little trouble getting used to living in Sammie's new mansion. Everything was like a dream to him.

"Benjamin, you'd better get used to being a millionaire. What I have is half yours."

Summer was over, and Sammie and Benjamin started their second year of college at Florida State University so that they could be close to the ranch.

Sammie and Benjamin loved going to the ranch most weekends. Benjamin wondered if he would ever get used to this new life of his.

Sammie's parents asked Benjamin's parents, the Crows, to come to Florida. They told Benjamin's father that they would have a good-paying job waiting for him and that Mrs. Lois Crow wouldn't need to work if she didn't want to.

The O'Grady's had that empty house in the nearby town of Rockledge that had all new furniture in it. The Cunninghams had lived in it for just a short time and later moved to the ranch. Now it had been vacant for a while, and that worried Simon a little.

The Crows did move to Rockledge, Florida, and they loved their new home. They were so pleased to be close to Benjamin and Sammie. They were also delighted getting to know the O'Grady's better. Simon O'Grady's hired Terry Crow to be a mechanic on the ranch because he was an excellent mechanic.

Sammie and Benjamin had finished college. Sammie was still getting used to being called Mrs. Sammie Crow. Benjamin was now helping run the farm and ranch. They planned on planting other things on the vast land that hadn't yet been utilized. Both Benjamin and Sammie added lemon trees, mango trees, and avocado trees. They researched all of these and wanted to try raising them all.

The new name of the citrus ranch was now the O'Grady, Klein, and Crow Citrus Ranch. The Ranch never looked better. Sammie was so happy to have been a part of fulfilling her grandfather's dreams.

Sammie represented her father, *Cody*. Kate represented her late husband, *Davis,* Last of all, *Simon*, Sammie's uncle, who was the youngest son of Samuel O'Grady. They all ran the ranch together. All of Samuel O'Grady's sons were represented by one of his family. It was always Samuel's wish to pass the ranch on to the next generations, and it had happened.

Sammie's life had been full of twists and turns, and now all of her dreams had come true. Benjamin and Sammie had three daughters and four sons. Benjamin reminded Sammie that there still would be challenges ahead for them, but together, they would handle them.

CPSIA information can be obtained
at www.ICGtesting.com
Printed in the USA
BVHW032034281019
562291BV00005B/19/P